THREE-LEGGED HORSE

A JUSTIN BODEAN WESTERN

THREE-LEGGED HORSE

RUSS HALL

FIVE STAR
A part of Gale, Cengage Learning

GALE
CENGAGE Learning·

Farmington Hills, Mich • San Francisco • New York • Waterville, Maine
Meriden, Conn • Mason, Ohio • Chicago

LIBRARY OF CONGRESS CATALOGING-IN-PUBLICATION DATA

Hall, Russ, 1949–
    Three-legged horse : a Justin Bodean western / Russ Hall. —
First edition.
    pages ; cm
    ISBN 978-1-4328-3065-6 (hardcover) — ISBN 1-4328-3065-1
(hardcover) — ISBN 978-1-4328-3063-2 (ebook) — ISBN 1-4328-
3063-5 (ebook)
    I. Title.
PS3558.A37395T48 2015
813'.54—dc23   2015012956

First Edition. First Printing: October 2015
Find us on Facebook– https://www.facebook.com/FiveStarCengage
Visit our website– http://www.gale.cengage.com/fivestar/
Contact Five Star™ Publishing at FiveStar@cengage.com

Printed in the United States of America
1 2 3 4 5 6 7 19 18 17 16 15

THREE-LEGGED HORSE

CHAPTER ONE

The ripping blast of the first gunshot burst louder in their ears than any crack of a bullwhip. The sound of the driver letting go of the reins as he fell forward into the heels of the galloping horses raised every eyebrow inside the stagecoach. That sat them all up straight and had the men reaching for the window curtains. Nothing to see out there but the black of night.

"Bullock? You okay up there?" one of the men yelled.

Pale yellow light from a candle in a cage that swung frantically to the left and right with the pitching of the thoroughbrace coach dimmed until Justin could barely see the faces of the others.

Bullock's shotgun boomed once, then again. His boots sounded on the board as he slid over from where he'd been riding guard to where he must have bent to grab at the loose reins.

Inside the roughly jostling stagecoach, the dim flame swayed even harder back and forth, showing a range of frightened and determined faces before banging into one side just as the next shot blew the cage and candle apart and snuffed the light, throwing bits of wood and metal across all five passengers and leaving them in the pitch dark.

A shot lanced out from inside the coach, its yellow-orange flame and the smell of powder filling the air.

"Don't shoot back. You'll get us all killed."

"Oh, Lordy."

Two more thuds of lead slammed into the side of the coach. For a moment the gallop of the horses steadied. Bullock must've gotten hold of the reins. Another shot cracked the night apart and the reins went loose. The horses, wild with fear, kicked up their heels in earnest as they started down a hill. The coach swayed back and forth harder, tilting farther each time. The slightest curve would send the whole thing tumbling, and the road had been nothing but curves for the past several miles.

The four horses kicked up in wild stampede. All of the passengers sat in inky black, but that didn't keep them from imagining the wide startled eyes and flared nostrils as the frantic hooves kicked up rocks along the path while bullets whined and ricocheted around the coach.

A sudden lurch and drag signaled one of the horses taking a bullet hard enough to drop it. The other horses, held captive by the tack, snapped under the momentum of the coach bearing down on them as it headed down a steep grade. The whole thing pitched hard left, then right, suddenly falling into a tumble that flipped the coach onto one side, then its top, finally to crash clear over on its other side. Inside, the passengers tumbled over and over in a tangle of grasping, screaming humans.

When the stagecoach at last slid all the way to a stop, the inside of the coach fell silent. Outside, one horse whinnied in pain, another made a low desperate snort as it tried to rise until the sound of approaching hooves was followed by two gunshots. The horses lay quiet now too and no longer tugged at the leather rigging that held them to the ground.

Low voices accompanied the short work of prying loose the locked money-and-mail box and sifting through the tumble of luggage. Then the men climbed back on their horses with what truck they could handle. The clicking of their horses' hooves faded in the distance before anyone inside the tumbled wreck of the coach began to stir.

★ ★ ★ ★ ★

"Well, they've sure enough gone and kilt our fancy lady." The coarse-as-leather cowhand passenger, Lucas Brent, straightened up from beside where the woman lay stretched out. The woman had an almost pretty face that looked peaceful in death, though the blood on her dress confirmed she had died by violence. Lucas, like the rest of them, had tumbled around inside the coach but hadn't taken a bullet. His shirt was torn in a couple of places and his hat wasn't all the way back into the shape it had been, but his buckskin leather vest had taken the fall well.

The horizon to the east was a dim yellow line. But it provided enough light to see the extent of damage. The stagecoach lay partially on its top and split open like a cracked egg. The horses, two roans, a bay, and a dappled gray, all lay dead in their traces, two of them with bullet holes in their heads.

"And it don't look like it'll be long before Mister Bodean there sheds his mortal coil and joins her," Lucas added.

Justin's head snapped up from where the man of the cloth was helping tend to his father, who lay stretched out with his head resting on a small rise of flat rock. "Don't talk about Pa like that. There's still hope," he shouted.

"Keep your voice down, boy. There are Indians out here." The voice was soft, belying the size of the speaker, Francis Marion Gallagher, who, at six-foot-six and as big around as a live oak, was the biggest man Justin had ever seen. The command was also unlike him so far. He had been nothing but talkative and loud so far. Back east Justin had heard the word bellicose used, and it could fit Francis—at least if that means having a belly and a booming voice brought on by much self-confidence. Francis and Lucas had bickered at each other nonstop for most of the trip. But now his voice sounded hushed, and he glanced about with narrowed eyes to the tops of hills and mesas around them. He was a well-dressed man, sporting a suit made of a burgundy velvet cloth that would have suited a fop better than a man of his robust size. He had come out of the roll of the stagecoach without a thread out of place, though he had loosened the matching burgundy silk scarf that had been tied at the throat of his store-bought white shirt. A white silk handkerchief hung loose out of his breast pocket.

"Them Injuns are mostly wiped out, skedaddled where they ain't plain licked and sent off to a reservation," Lucas said. "They's only a few renegades and mavericks of them left who don't know their days are over, or who don't care."

Justin should have felt calmer at hearing that, but he kept a wary eye on the tops of the surrounding hills all the same, expecting Indians or more robbers to pop up at any time. Lucas seemed like a fellow who knew these parts, knew them well and the hard way. His lips looked dry and cracked enough to bear witness to long sessions in the saddle under an unforgiving sun. Dust lay deep in the folds of his worn clothes, and his only luggage had been the considerably experienced saddle, bedroll, and saddlebags he'd lashed to the top of the stagecoach beside some of the other luggage. He wore a hat that had been black once, though it had since grown paler from a dried sweat line that went halfway up to the crown and out into the now-wrinkled brim.

"Well, we're a ways from water and the nearest chance of getting any, unless you have ideas about that," Francis said. He slid a flask out of his back pocket and took a sip, a trickle of red from the wine easing from the corner of his mouth until he licked it clean before it headed down into the thick black stubble that covered his chin.

Lucas glanced up toward the outline of a red-tailed hawk soaring high above them, out on an early morning hunt. It wasn't a buzzard, but they would be along soon enough. "I know about thirst. Was out in the desert once."

"That makes you an expert?"

"On the third day we still couldn't get outta the sun and there was no water at all. We had to cut the throat of one of the burros and drink its blood."

"I'd like just once to hear a story of one of you dust-born cowpoke fellows that doesn't involve you drinking blood, eating your own belt, or drinking out of a muddy hoofprint." Francis's voice had risen in spite of himself. He was a man who had a room-filling voice most of the time, and it was hard for him to hold back. He caught himself and looked around.

Justin stayed crouched low beside his father, whose breathing was ragged but steady, although every once in a while he'd give a lurch and press his eyes shut tight. Unlike the lady who had been sitting on the other side of Justin and who was probably dead the moment a bullet had found her, Justin's father had tumbled half out the door of the stage as it had smashed end-over-end on the rocks. Dried blood caked his ears and nose, and his face had taken on a purple hue. Justin couldn't imagine what life would be like without him. He looked up and swept the area around them—not much to see: yellow and red rocks among the bare limestone showing through the hills that were sprinkled with the green dots of yucca and prickly pear cactus. They were somewhere in the tail end of Texas hill country on or near the Llano Estacado, the staked plains, where he had heard the last holdout renegades of the Comanche still roamed.

The preacher finished saying a few words over the fallen flower, if that cowhand was to be believed about her. She wore a dress made of red silk and lace, so he might have been right about her. All Justin knew was that she had sure felt good to his shoulder as the coach had swayed from side to side, causing the passengers to nudge against each other during the early going in the coach. She had smelled plenty good too. His own mother had died long enough ago he had only wispy memories of her, just enough to be glad she hadn't come along on this journey. "Adventure," his dad had said to him. "A change. A chance at something new." Well, they were having that with bells on.

As the man in the dark suit with the square splash of white at the front collar stood, the cowhand, Lucas, looked down at the lady and said, "Shame about her. She could have entertained us out here."

"I doubt she would have anything to do with you, even if you bathed. So I'd put that past your thoughts and regrets," Francis said. He looked to be a man used to having his say, or one not accustomed to having to wait for a reply or rebuttal. The words he and Lucas had been trading on the trip had at first been in jest, and then a bitter edge began to show. It seemed clear Francis thought himself a better man.

Lucas looked like he had an opinion about that, but kept his thoughts to himself. Francis, though finely dressed, stood a half head taller and looked like he could wrestle a bear to good advantage. Lucas went around to the back of the stagecoach to poke through the rubble there. An open bandbox lay next to an old Maltese colored trunk with a cover with the furs still on. There was a brass-studded leather trunk next to a staved-in barrel that lay on its side. He found his saddlebags next to his saddle and took out a gun belt, unrolled it from around the holster and strapped it on. As soon as he wore it, he took on a more confident look.

Francis, though, ignored him. He took his silver flask out again, lifted it to his mouth and tilted it back until it was empty. He shook it and looked inside. Frowning, he went back to the spilled luggage until he found the barrel, its side smashed in and the rocks and sand around it stained red. He rocked back a step. "Oh, those low-life, sidewinding, claim-jumping sons of"—he glanced toward Justin—"sea snakes. That was burgundy, mind you, shipped all the way from Paris frog-hop France."

He looked around at the rest of the scattered mess. His eyes darted through the loose trunks and gear until he spotted the woman's carpet bag. "She'd have one," he muttered and rushed for the bag, tugged it open and dug inside until he found what he was looking for. He came out with a pearl-handled derringer, dwarfed in his huge hand.

Lucas's hand slid down his side until it hovered near his low-slung holster. But Francis didn't even glance his way. He rushed up to the nearest high patch of rocks and stood looking off in the direction the men who'd robbed the stage had ridden. "You sons of . . . heathen scum," he yelled. His next few words were lost in the blast of the small derringer as he fired off both rounds into the air in that direction.

The preacher had crouched down again beside Justin's dad. He looked up, staring at Francis. Lucas was as surprised himself, and bewildered.

"Well, that was certainly a lot of tomfoolishness." The words rasped, but had an edge of bite to them. Justin looked down, surprised his father had spoken.

"If you weren't a dying man, I might take offense," Francis said, looking down at the gun that was tiny in his hand. He seemed surprised to find it there.

"You get around to thinking of anyone but your own worthless self, you let us know, okay?" It was as far as Dad got before he gave a low cough. The preacher wiped at blood from the corner of his mouth with a handkerchief and helped him painfully bend to one side so he could spit.

Francis looked around them, more carefully now, as if realizing for the first time how much they would indeed be buzzard bait unless things changed. The horses were dead. None of them knew how far the next station or town was. The driver and guard were dead. They had no water. He spoke out loud without looking at any of the others. "If I'd written this mess, I'd sure enough planned a way out for us. Just wait. You'll see."

"Foolishness," Justin's father muttered, though his voice was fading.

"I should take you to task for that," Francis muttered, as if he were the only one who had a gun, though Lucas was armed now and hadn't wasted any bullets. The preacher too wore a gun high on his right side. That had been what worried Justin, niggled at his head. In all the ruckus, he hadn't seen who had fired shots out the window from inside the coach. He slipped his hand down to feel his father's gun, and it felt cool to his touch. It wasn't like him to take incautious shots anyway.

"You can cry in your blasted silk handkerchief for all I care," his dad said. Justin wished he wouldn't egg the man on so. Lucas and Francis had been squabbling most of the ride to here, and now his dad was setting in against the man. Francis could get on your nerves with all his loud talk and high-tone ways.

"It happens that my handkerchief is indeed silk." Francis glanced down at the flash of white on his chest.

"Figures. Give it over," the preacher said.

"What for?"

"I'm trying to save a man's life is why."

"He's past saving."

Justin felt a red flush of anger stir up inside him and shoot all the way up his neck to his head. The next thing he knew he had leaped halfway to his feet and felt the preacher holding him back while he screamed, "I've about had it from you."

Francis looked perplexed. His expression didn't change when he saw that Lucas had his gun drawn and pointed at him. "Give the man your stupid hanky."

"Well, okay. Sure." It was the first contrition Justin had heard from the man since they had found themselves in this mess.

14

From the look on Francis's face you would have thought his best friends had turned on him, though with his constant loud and boastful talking he could hardly number any of them as his friends. Now, for the first time, everyone's true colors were showing, yet as Justin watched, he could see the man's amazing self-confidence wrestle itself back into place on his oversized face.

While the preacher dabbed the blood away from Justin's father's chin, Justin asked Francis, "What makes you so sure we're going to get out of this?"

Francis was busy digging in the lady's bag again. At first Justin thought he was after money. Then his hand came out with a fistful of bullets. He loaded the derringer and slipped it into the side pocket of his suit pants. He dropped the loose bullets into the other side. Doing so seemed to restore his earlier bluster.

"If you've ever read the adventures of that six-gun legend Tornado Trey Calvin, then you'd know why. I write those stirring yarns and know more about the Wild West myself than you might think. I'd be surprised if you haven't read one or two. Anyone with a dime can, though you have to be able to read." He glanced toward Lucas.

"I've read one or two," Justin admitted. "But they were written by a fella named Ben Blunt."

"That's me. That's the penname, the *non de plume* I use." Francis continued to ignore Lucas's drawn gun. He took his flask out of his back pocket, frowned at it, and nearly tossed it away before he thought better of it and tucked it back into his pocket.

"If you're done swaggering and jawing for all you're worth, why don't you close your mouth and do something about cleaning up here, and seeing what we can use," the preacher said. "You, put your gun up," he said to Lucas. The way he snapped, and the fact he wore a gun, made Justin wonder about him again. Had he been the one shooting out the window? Then the preacher said, "We might be here a spell, and we have to do something about burying these dead."

Justin's head snapped down to his dad, and he realized for the first time his dad was no longer breathing.

Buzzards had begun to circle in earnest by early afternoon, even though they had managed rock pile graves for the dead, even for Justin's father. He had strapped on his father's gun, feeling like the worst kind of thief for doing so. The preacher had said a few words. Then they had gathered in what shade the crumpled coach provided and had huddled close to keep away from the relentless sun in the cloudless sky.

Adventure. Justin's dad had told him often that things would be different if they went west where everyone could start anew. Well, his dad probably wasn't the first to think so. It sure sounded silly to Justin now, sitting there in the dirt with his back to the crushed side of the coach. There wasn't anything they could do about the horses. Flies were thick around them now. When the gusting wind blew, the thick smell of the dead horses swept over them, and all they could do was sit and wait for something to happen.

It seemed futile to wait, but they could hardly walk off in the direction the two thin ruts of the road headed and hope a town was only a day or two ahead. Justin didn't know what to think, or who to trust. True enough, it had been the cowpoke earlier who had given him a nudge and said, "Come on. I'll help you burry your pa."

That burly writer fellow had pitched in too and helped, though he seemed to do it because it was expected of him, not because he truly cared a hoot about any of them. Justin couldn't begin to figure him out. It was hard not to like him in some strange way. Admiring him was another thing altogether. He rubbed almost everyone the wrong way, yet there was something fascinating about him. One minute he was brash and full of himself, the next he was looking around in a way that had far less bluster in it. But strong? The man was a giant. When they had to get the coach off the dead guard Bullock, Francis had lifted a whole side by himself while the other two men scooped out the guard. After letting the coach drop back to the ground, he had straightened and brushed himself off as if he'd done nothing more than hoist a bale of hay.

He'd hiked the short way back up the road and carried the dead stage driver over his shoulder like he was a sack of flour. But now that they were preparing to bury the dead, at least enough to keep the coyotes from having a go at them, they all looked about with heightened apprehension. They had agreed to start walking as soon as the sun began to settle. Then Justin would get a chance to see how brave he really was, what with robbers, Indians, and who knew what ahead, with no water and only a few guns and limited ammo. The robbers had taken the stage's shotgun and Francis, big as he was, had only the lady's belly gun.

When they had the shallow holes ready for the driver, guard, fancy lady, and Justin's father, Justin let them start on the others while he bent close over his father. He took the watch and chain, with a small penknife as its fob, out of his father's pocket. The wallet he kept was flatter than he expected. He glanced to the others. They were busy, the preacher saying a few words as the other two men made a small mound of rocks. Justin opened the penknife and bent close, lifted his father's jacket and ran the knife blade across the stitching at the bottom of the lining. He glanced again, then reached in and pulled out a stiff piece of paper, folded it and slipped it quickly into his own pocket.

When he looked up, he thought he saw Francis looking at him. Maybe he'd imagined that, because they were all busy lowering the next body into a hole when he looked again.

He wanted to say something to his father. "I forgive you." But it didn't come. He stood, dusted off his pants, and took a few steps away while the others finished the grave they stood over and turned to move closer to Justin's father.

There were all silent now, waiting. The last thing anyone had said in a while was when the preacher nudged Justin and said, "It's okay. Go ahead and cry, Justin." But he didn't want to cry, or couldn't, and didn't know which was worse. His insides felt as twisted and drawn as a piece of wet rawhide drying in the sun.

Dad would never get a chance to prove or fail to prove he was a brave man. Justin should feel sad, he told myself. He was glad his father had spoken up to the others the way he had, even when he'd been lying there dying. But Justin was all too aware that words and deeds don't always match. Back home in Baltimore, Pa had been a loud and bold talker, pounding his chest, if needed, and stretching a few yarns.

When a rapist and killer had been caught right in their neighborhood everyone heard him. He'd been plenty loud about that. "Why, they ought to string him up, and draw and quarter him after that." He'd described some of the most gruesome ends Justin could imagine for that fellow. But he had sung considerably smaller when Justin was nine and they came upon a burglar going through their house. The fellow pulled a knife, and that's when Justin got to see the real insides of Dad. He'd dropped to his knees, pleading, while the burglar had grabbed Justin's ma's hair and killed her right in front of them. It was a messy, awful scene, but Justin hadn't cared because he expected to die too.

The burglar hadn't even bothered with Dad, as if he wasn't worth the bother. But when he went for Ma's necklace, Justin rushed to pull her away from him. "You're sure a game one," the burglar had said, and winked. He hit Justin on the head with the butt end of his knife. He didn't do anything to Justin's dad. He didn't have to, or thought it was beneath him. Dad had been, oh, so brave when it came to talk. But that hadn't saved Mom. Justin's biggest fear of all, though, didn't have so much to do with his dad but whether or not he had inherited or been infected with that sort of lack of courage.

He drew his dad's gun from the holster at his side and checked the cylinder. All the bullets were there. The gun hadn't been fired. Who had been shooting from the inside of the coach, then?

They sat there, side by side, those of them who had survived: Francis, Lucas, the preacher, and Justin. They surveyed the fading hills around them, expecting who knew what—anything but someone riding to their aid.

The man of the cloth suddenly spoke for the first time in a while. He had a low, powerful voice, something like the clap of doom, and it made each word hit like a blacksmith's hammer blow onto an anvil. "We each, in the end, are measured, and in a way that only our God and we ourselves will know." He closed his mouth and the words echoed among the buzz of flies on the dead horses and the silent circling of the buzzards. The cowhand looked thoroughly disgusted and added nothing. The well-dressed writer seemed absorbed in his own thoughts as well.

Justin's hand slid down to rest on his father's pistol. He was the man of the family now, and as far as he knew, the last living member of it. He expected to feel sad, but couldn't. Instead, he felt angry, alone and afraid, and just a bit guilty. The confusion didn't help him in a situation that was hard to comprehend in the first place.

He had plenty to think over as he waited along with the others for the sun to eventually settle in the west. The heat never let up, and trickles of sweat ran down his neck. He began to itch powerfully for water. They had found none when they rummaged through what was left of the luggage scattered around the coach. What he had found preyed on his mind. It was a scrap of paper, a torn part of a telegraph form. The part that that showed who it was to, or who had sent it, was missing. The only part of the message left was "I want you to ruin the man."

Justin was certain it hadn't been sent to him or his father, which made him all the more cautious about saying anything to the other three men who sweated beside him in the slim shade, waiting for the dark.

It had been quiet too long. He finally spoke. "Why do you say she was a fancy lady?"

Francis chuckled, and the cowhand slid a slow hand across his face, a hand so dry the stubble on his chin crackled.

"I wouldn't worry your head none about that just now. She dressed fine. Let it go at that." This came from the preacher, a preacher who wore a gun.

"That's the way of religion, son. Cloak with mystery that which is too human to ignore." Francis's voice had begun to rasp since there was no more of his red wine with which to oil it.

"Take talk lightly, son, from a man who trades in lies for his living," the preacher said.

"Oh, now I'm a liar, am I?" Francis started to push himself upright.

"Aw, sit down," the cowhand said. "You said yourself a while back that this was your first time west."

"That's right. Those words you spew all come from second-hand information, and they don't give you any grounds to dispute religion." The preacher's right hand rested on the butt of his gun, Justin noticed.

Either the heat or the fact he wasn't as well-armed as the preacher made Francis slow and then flop back to where he'd sat to stew in his own indignation. His earlier bluster was subdued, as if it had been from the wine he'd drawn his strength or courage, the way Sampson of old had been with his hair. With the wine all gone, Francis was tamer, though Justin could still see him bending an iron bar almost double, as if by accident, while prying loose one of the coach's corners from the rock that held it. Then bending it again with his hands until it was straight. Using the bar as a lever to lift the stage had failed, which was when Francis had just lowered himself at one corner and lifted the whole thing by hand.

Talk of religion only served to remind Justin that they were all likely to die out here, just like his father had. The black buzzards above circled around and around in the pale cloudless sky.

"I imagine you miss your father dearly," the preacher said. "Try to dwell upon all the things he did for you in your years together."

"He saw that I ate and had a place to sleep, and that I got a middling education. But there was a lot Pa didn't do as much as he did." The bitterness that had crept into Justin's tone should have shocked him, but letting go of it felt like freeing a bird. He knew how he'd felt when his mother died, and of his father's failure at the time. Justin hadn't before faced the stark disappointment he held for his father, nor had he needed to until now.

"Perhaps, then," the preacher said, "you should think of the many things you have done for him."

Justin's voice broke when he went to speak. "What have I done? Nothing. I guess I . . ."

"You did something for your pa many of us don't have the

chance at," the cowhand said. "You helped bury him."

"And you have the chance at something else too," Francis said. "You can avenge him."

That brought talking to a halt for a spell. Justin had much to stew about, but as the day wore on, his thoughts gravitated to how much he would like a drink of water, cool or warm, clear or even muddy.

"Reckon we'll have to walk as far ahead as we can in the dark," the preacher finally said. The sun still seemed quite a number of hours from reaching the horizon.

The cowhand was looking down at his boots, more fit for going on horseback than for long walks. He nodded slowly. "Yep."

"Man, I'm parched," Francis said.

"You 'bout ready to drink water from that hoofprint now?"

"No. Though I can't believe no one has come along to give us a hand," Francis said.

"Just as well it ain't Comanche. I think we're in what was buffalo-eating land, though it could be the antelope eaters or yap eaters for all I know or care. We'll be just as dead, and scalped, with one group as another." The cowhand was on the far end of the row from Francis, so the writer had to lean out to glare that way.

"I didn't know there were so many kinds of Comanche," Justin said.

"There's only one kind of Comanche, and that's the kind we don't want to run into, the kind likely to put an arrow into you," Francis said.

"Listen to the Yankee expert. Don't even know most of them have guns of one sort or another by now."

"Will you two just shut up a spell," the preacher finally said.

Francis started to say something, but the cowhand held up a hand to stop him. He eased his back away from the coach's side and bent an ear toward the two-wheel path leading up the hill they'd tumbled down when the coach had wrecked.

Justin concentrated until he could hear it too—the steady clicking of hooves on the road, and they were coming their way.

"Yeah," the cowhand said, drawing his gun. "And them ain't shod horses neither."

"Indians?" Francis whispered, reaching into one suit jacket pocket for the derringer.

Not much of a weapon unless the fighting gets real close, Justin figured, reaching down for his own pistol grip.

The hooves clicked closer their way.

CHAPTER TWO

Three horses came over the rise, rode right down the middle of the stagecoach road coming at them. Justin's heart shot up into his throat. Indians. He glanced toward the cowhand. Lucas nodded. Yep. Comanche.

The lead rider rode a paint horse. Hard to tell about the horses that flanked the leader. They could be cavalry horses or someone's livestock. All three of the riders carried long guns. Justin caught the sly movements as the preacher and Lucas both eased their hands toward the hilts of their pistols. Francis had sneaked the derringer out of his pocket and started to raise his arm. The preacher had his gun out of its holster. Justin had an idea by now of who'd fired a gun from inside the coach. Before the preacher could raise his pistol to point it, Lucas glanced behind them. "Pssst."

When the preacher glanced his way, Lucas jerked his head toward their backs. Justin's head swung with the others. An Indian sat his horse right behind them, his bow drawn and the full length of an arrow pointed right at the preacher's back. Another Comanche came up behind him, raised what looked like an old muzzle loader at them.

The preacher's hand lowered until his gun hung at his side. By the time Justin looked forward again, two more Comanche had ridden into place on either flank, a little farther back. It looked as close to a military maneuver as Justin had ever heard about, though he had only read accounts.

Seven Indians. They had them surrounded. Inside, Justin wanted to scream at the others not to give up, but to draw their guns and fight. They were going to be killed anyway, based on every tale he'd ever read. He'd rather handily forgotten that he was wearing a gun too. He looked down at it, as if it had betrayed him.

As they rode closer, Justin would have been hard pressed to tell what the other Comanche warriors looked like. His eyes stayed fixed on the one in the center who led them. Dressed in buckskin shirt and leggings, worn and tattered at the ends from much hard use, and such that he also wore a breechcloth, since the pants mostly covered just the legs, like chaps. He wore beaded moccasins on his feet. His hair hung in thick black braids on either side of his head, and a single feather hung from his head, and it was bent midway, as if he'd fallen on it.

The man's face was hard, far more rugged than any of the white men, more rugged than the long stretch of road that lay ahead. The black onyx of his eyes glittered in a suppressed eagerness of burning coals as he looked them over, while the rest of his face stayed stern as stone. He rode his horse like an extension of his own body, easy and free, but in complete control. Justin swallowed hard, seeing himself and the other men as bodies strewn beside the fallen coach. He believed right that moment he was taking his last breaths on this earth.

As the surrounding Comanche group got all the way up to them, they all raised weapons. Justin froze, fought the temptation to close his eyes, then had to take a deep gasp of air upon realizing he'd been holding his breath, waiting for the flurry of shots. The leader nodded for the men to throw their pistols aside. Justin watched each of them, expecting one of them to take a chance and try to get off a shot that would have started their last moment. None did. They all tossed their pistols to the side, Justin too. Francis's tiny derringer making a small clatter as it landed on one of the revolvers. The leader nodded toward Lucas. Two of the other Comanche moved closer, led him out of sight.

A couple of the Comanche poked through the litter from the crushed stagecoach, picking through anything they might use, then went to the horses, started cutting out chunks of meat from them.

Justin began to shake as he stood, as if from ague or a deep chill. They led the preacher away next. Finally they took Francis. Each time Justin waited to hear a shot. Maybe they were cutting throats, taking scalps. He heard pounding thuds, but no shots. Were they beating their heads in? He tried not to see any of it in his head. Had the thought been to take the strongest, most dangerous first? He had little doubt they were all going to die, wherever they were being led. The Comanche had not yet said a single word or made a sound. Justin tried as hard as he could not to cry out or even make a sound. But he nearly made an inadvertent peep when he stood alone at last and they came back to him and started to lead him away.

He stepped over the litter of the tumbled stagecoach, skirted the graves, and went over a rise of rocks. On the other side the land stretched out in a flat sandy stretch of hard packed dirt. Lucas, Francis, and the preacher all lay there, stretched out, nude, their ankles and hands tied to stakes driven into the ground. A pile of their clothes lay off to one side. The Comanche nearest Justin waved the end of his rifle, a worn and weathered Sharps carbine, at Justin, who got the idea. He began to take off his clothes, toss each item onto the pile.

They stretched him out on the ground that felt rough and rasped at Justin's back, tied rawhide strips to his wrists and ankles, and pounded in the stakes around him, using a large flat rock as their hammer. The ground was already warm. Then they stepped away from him, their departing shadows taking away any shade. The sun beat down on him. It was going to get a whole lot hotter. None of them had had as much as a sip of water. His mouth felt dry and parched, perhaps more so from realizing what lay ahead.

The Indians went through his things, as they must have done the others, ignored his watch and the money in the wallet. Meant nothing to them. They moved out of sight. This close to the ground, he could hear the sound of their hooves as they moved away. That was it. They had left them there to die in the sun.

"Why didn't they just kill us?" Justin croaked, his throat already starting to feel sandy and dry.

"They want us to suffer," the preacher said. "This will take longer than just killing us."

"Why?" Justin's voice came out as a near squeak.

"You don't know anything about Antelope Hills then, do you?"

"That was Bent Feather himself, was it?" Lucas said.

By bending his neck Justin could look toward each of them as they spoke. He avoided looking at their bodies, though he caught just enough to see they were all white as parchment. Wouldn't stay that way for long. Francis, for a rare stretch of time had stayed silent, which was quite unlike him. He seemed to be soaking in what the others were saying.

Justin heard a scramble of raspy scales across the sand. His head snapped the other direction. Just a lizard coming out from a clump of prickly pear cactus to have a look around.

"Yep." The preacher's voice was starting to sound a little dry too. It wouldn't be long for any of them, stretched out like this in the sun, like jerky being dried. "When Governor Runnels put ol' Rip Ford in charge of a bunch of hellions made up of Rangers, militia and Tonks, he really laid into those Comanche villages."

"Tonks?" Justin couldn't help himself.

"Tonkawas." Lucas had to clear his voice to speak. "Injuns that grew friendly to the whites."

The preacher ignored the interruption. "The Indians in the territories, the Comancheria in particular, were supposed to be left alone by federal troops. But with settlers wanting to move in where the Indians were taking up space, Runnels sent in Rip Ford. The Rip came from the way he signed casualty reports with RIP for 'Rest in Peace.' And there were casualties."

"Ford was a bloody murderer, wasn't he?" Francis finally spoke.

"He figured that the way Comanche worked when dealing with settlers was to kill every male, take the kids as captives to grow up in the tribe, and to rape the women old enough for that. So Ford had to be just as vicious. He trumped them, is what he did. When he laid into them he killed everything, right down to the village dogs."

Justin thought he heard a lot of eager pride in the preacher's voice.

"You weren't one of those Rangers who rode with him, were you?" Lucas asked.

"Before I took to the book, indeed I was."

"So you have one riled-up Comanche who left us out here this way to die," Francis said. "Is that the way of it?"

"He was one of the few survivors. Rip Ford and the Tonk chief, Placido, ripped into sleeping villages and went through the lodges like a fire. At Little Robe Creek the village at least wasn't sleeping, but the Comanche lost their chief in that one, old Iron Jacket. Bent Feather was his youngest son, who was away from the village when it happened. He came back to find the scraps of what little was left of his wife and children. Iron Jacket's oldest son, Peta Noncona, nearly drew Ford and the others into a trap where he meant to pay them back plenty. But

Ford backed off, burnt everything behind him, and cut out of there. Then when the War Between the States began, the feds pulled out all the Union troops. That left the settlers at the mercy of some mighty angry Comanche and Kiowa, and even a few Apache who'd joined in. They thought they were winning, that they'd won. They found out different, and most of them have been wiped out. But Bent Feather there is a remnant, a renegade who just don't know the meaning of the word quit."

"We're just lucky it wasn't Tonks who came across us," Lucas said.

"Why? Because you might've heard they have a taste for long pig, and we might have been roasting ourselves now instead of those Injuns just packing along some horse flesh? I heard those rumors all the way back east. I heard just as many tales the other way, that there was nothing to it." Francis's usual bluster-ing calm started to show the edge of agitation. Waiting in the growing heat of the sun to die can do that to someone.

"I thought you said your publisher sent you all the way out here to learn how things really are?" the preacher said.

"That's true enough."

"Well, the first thing you need to throw out is anything you *think* you already know; what you learnt back there. The Tonk may be a lot of things, but I never saw any of them with a taste for that kind of flesh. I stood right beside our Tonkawa sharpshooter Jim Pockmark when he sent a bullet from his Sharps buffalo rifle right through Iron Jacket's old Spanish armor. Those Tonks took a lot of grisly souvenirs, but I never saw them cook up or eat anything they took as a trophy. Best not to speak ill of what you don't know. Tell you this, though. If it was Tonks had come across us, we'd be flat-out dead right now. Bent Feather's burning a slower fire and would rather let the sun do the work, all day if need be."

"I get it. He's one angry Indian." Francis was tugging at his bindings, as they all had tried. "I, for one, am tired of this. I don't intend to lie here and get baked, whether anyone's going to be around to enjoy steaks off me or not."

"It was a long time ago." The preacher's voice had grown tired, accepting of his fate. "But he's still plenty riled."

"You seem to know damn all about this. You were Ford's lieutenant, weren't you?" Francis's voice was strained as he tugged at his bonds. "You're lucky he didn't recognize you."

"I said it was long ago, and he never saw me, though his brother did."

"Been hiding behind the cloth since, eh?" Francis surged again. No go.

Justin tried tugging at the rawhide strips that bound him. Not a single budge. They seemed to be drying and tightening, getting stronger rather than weaker.

He could see the others trying to get loose as well. No success.

"I would like the chance just once to try and walk out of this," Justin said. "To do something. Maybe make it to a town."

"You wouldn't have any more chance of doing that, all on your own, than a three-legged horse," Lucas said. He also seemed to be resigned to looking at the end of his days.

"I . . . am . . . tired . . . of . . . this!" Francis's growl progressed into a shouting roar.

He flexed his bulk, arching his back and pulling with all he had.

Justin watched, fascinated. Any second he expected the big man to explode. Francis's face turned red, then nearly purple. His back arched. His muscles bulged.

"Grrrrrr." The right stake quivered in the ground, then popped loose.

Francis relaxed, rested for just a second, then reached across and pulled the other stake out of the ground.

Justin knew how deep and well-pounded into the ground those stakes had been. He'd tried with everything he had, and his stakes hadn't moved the tiniest bit.

Francis sat up. He tugged the stakes loose that held his feet. Then he stood and, still naked, went over to Lucas and the preacher and pulled their stakes out of the ground with his hands. Lucas came over to Justin and tried to get him loose. Francis was digging through the pile of clothing, seeking out his own. Lucas had to go to the pile, find his belt knife, which the Indians apparently hadn't wanted. He used it to cut himself free from the rawhide thongs that had held him and had turned his hands a bright pink. Then he cut Justin loose. Francis and the preacher both came to him to have him cut away the leather from their limbs.

All of them spent the next few moments getting dressed, rubbing at their wrists the while.

"Well, I know what the Comanche look like close up now," Francis grumbled. He searched and couldn't find his velvet jacket. "Looks like one of them thieving Comanche have made off with that."

"You didn't notice that at least two of the Injuns riding with Bent Feather were Kiowa?" Lucas tugged on his boots. He was fortunate that Indians almost never have any use for boots.

"No. You don't say." Francis did find his silver flask, which had sustained a small ding or two. Still usable, but nothing to put in it at the moment. The Comanches had no use for the tiny derringer when they'd taken the other guns, so he picked it up. He rubbed at his wrists more than the others, the natural color just only now coming back into his hands.

Justin watched him, trying hard to imagine what kind of strength it had taken to pull loose those stakes from the ground, hammered in so deep and hard that Lucas hadn't been able to pry one loose with both hands.

31

Justin found his father's watch. They hadn't wanted that, or the wallet. Good. He felt around, pulled the folded paper out. He was tempted to open it and take a look inside, make sure it had not been harmed. But again he thought he caught Francis watching him, so he quickly slipped it back into his pocket. Justin pulled on his boots, and he was wearing all that was left of his world.

They all went back to the stagecoach. It lay just as crumpled and useless as ever. They picked through it for anything that might be useful. Not a bit of water or a canteen that hadn't been crushed. Lucas started to coil up the coach's whip and tie it to his belt, then decided against it and tossed it aside. Justin's hat was creased and torn, but his father's fit him. He wore that.

Flies formed a black mass over the horse from which the Indians had cut some meat for their supper. They'd taken the ribs off the upper side of two of the horses, and a hind quarter as well.

Hungry and needing water as much as they did, none of them were tempted by anything the dead horses might provide.

"That's everything?" the preacher said at last.

"Reckon so." Lucas gave the crumpled shell of the stagecoach one last going over. He saw nothing they needed or could use. "That's it."

They all turned and started down the two ruts of road that headed the direction the stage had been headed. The sun was still up full enough that they all wore hats.

Justin could feel the heat growing and bouncing up from the ground beneath them. It was going to be a long walk, and not a one of them had the least idea of what lay ahead or how far it would be until they came to a town, a settler's home, or anything.

CHAPTER THREE

The walk across this stretch of Texas was the longes
ever undertaken in his life. His feet hurt. His calves
sun beat down on him, and this Francis fellow talke
time.

Justin glanced toward Lucas and the preacher. T
miserable too. Both had probably ridden horses
than they'd walked anywhere.

The road led on ahead, bending little until it f
sight, over a rise. Behind the rise, mesas rose up to t
and the occasional clump of cactus dotted the sand
on one side, grassy brown waving slopes on the otl
looked robin's egg-shell blue with only the tiniest w
cloud streaked here and there. The only birds to
had the V wings of buzzards, and they seemed h
toward where the dead horses lay. At least they wei
around overhead.

"You know, you expect to see a tall saguaro cact
there. But you don't. That doesn't keep my publish
ting them on the covers of my books." Franci
expansive arm across the bleak surroundings.

"What the devil are you talking about now?"
Walking in boots meant for riding seemed to be a
quite a bit.

"Our penance for being saved by the likes c
preacher muttered.

"The saguaro cactus grows in Arizona. Don't know why body back east can ever figure that out. It's the details that ake the story. I doubt you've ever even seen one, Lucas, uns you've ridden farther west than I think."

"Nope. Unless it's like the cactus I fell on once with the seat my pants as a kid, I don't know it from my aunt Nellie's oomers." The cowhand looked like he would like to spit, but mouth was too dry for it.

"These cacti can get over a hundred years old and forty even ty feet tall."

"What do you take me for, a tomfool?"

Francis fortunately didn't answer that.

They walked in quiet for the better part of another mile, just crunch of rocks and rasp of sand on their boots. The ground s quite warm, reflecting the heat of the sun up at them. The ims of their hats were no defense against that reflected heat.

Justin had heard from his father was about how this land s supposed to be rich and ripe with opportunity, yet all he w now just looked bleak and hostile to him. Dirt, sand, scrub ints, and way too much wind. They plodded on.

Justin's mouth felt so dry, he was afraid to speak. He looked und. No change in the scenery, and certainly no town ahead, t even a settler's cabin. They did walk past the charred and ckened ground where one had been. Just the stones of the imney stuck up from the ground like a monument.

Francis let his steps move him closer to Justin. He leaned r, spoke in a soft voice. "Why don't you let me take a look at map?"

"What map?"

"The one you took out of the lining of your father's jacket."

"No."

"I'm just trying to help."

"Leave the kid alone." Lucas's voice sounded raspy now too.

"Look, I'm trying to help. Hell, I made half the maps people bought back there. It's one of the ways my publisher made money. Even put them on the right paper, weathered them up some. Folks who bought those aren't going to get close to anything more than fool's gold."

"You must feel pretty proud about that." The preacher managed a sneer.

With the tiny derringer tucked back into his pocket, Francis was the only one of them armed now. The others had their gun belts, but nothing in them, not even bullets. That didn't seem to bother Lucas or the preacher. No one was going to start shooting with just the few of them jawing along out in the middle of nowhere.

"Of course I'm not proud. But it meant getting by. I wouldn't want the kid to get his hopes up for nothing."

"And if it's not one of your fakes, then what?" Lucas said.

"Okay then, I won't look at the darned thing and let him know. Let it be on your head."

"Fine with me."

Justin was beginning to tire of walking, and his mouth felt too much like cotton for him to want to side with either one of them, as long as they left him alone. Sweat trickled down from both temples and a rivulet of it started down the middle of his back under his shirt.

"We've got to stop, take a break." Francis lowered himself into a crouch. He seemed to be breathing hard. Justin felt better at once, because he had been right on the verge of saying the same thing and had been fighting back the words for the last quarter mile. Inside he felt as dry as a tumbleweed. Big fellow like Francis had to be feeling even dryer.

"Hey, do you guys hear something? Stand still. I feel it in my feet." Justin stood still.

"I think the sun has gotten to you, son." But the preacher

looked about.

Francis rose to his feet again.

"By damn, he's right." Lucas looked around. Off to their far left they saw the beginnings of a cloud of dust rising from beyond the rise in that direction.

"Shouldn't we take cover?" Justin looked to each of them.

"If it was Injuns, they wouldn't be making a dust cloud like that." Lucas tried to spit, but had no ammo. His mouth barely made a sound at all.

"Who is it, then?" Francis was tallest. He rose on his toes, didn't seem to see anything.

"Best wait and see."

Justin saw the shapes of men on horseback in the middle of the dust cloud once it was closer. Hard to imagine what group of men would ride in a bunch like that. Didn't look to be herding cattle, and even outlaws probably didn't have that big of a gang.

The riding group seemed to see them and swung to head their way.

"Rangers," the preacher said as they grew closer. "Probably."

Justin's hand went down to his empty holster. Better hope that's who they were.

As they rode closer, he heard the preacher say, "Yep. Rangers."

He wasn't so sure himself, but something inside him stirred. He'd been that way as a boy, the time he'd seen a band, wanting to march along beside them. Maybe that was the major thing deep and yearning inside him, to be a part of something. He looked the men over closely as they closed the distance and rode up to a whirling dust cloud of a stop.

Some of the men wore long dusters, others didn't, and they were all covered with a near-white dust. They yanked off their hats and beat the dust off themselves. Up close, they didn't look like cavalry or anything Justin had ever imagined. No two of them wore the same thing, except for the round metal dot on their chests. They looked like a mix of cowhands and assorted scalawags. One of them rode up to the front, reminding Justin of how the Indians had done it, so you knew who the leader was right away.

"John Jacob Stubbs here," the leader said. "*Sergeant* Stubbs. You're a sorry lot."

"Water." Francis could barely croak it.

Stubbs waved to one of the men who rode closer and lowered down his canteen.

"Take it easy at first," Stubbs cautioned.

That didn't keep Francis from taking big gulping drinks when the canteen came to him. Justin took a small sip, then a bigger one. The water was warm and tasted stale, with a mix of leather or metal, but it was the best drink he'd ever had.

"Where're your mounts?" Stubbs waited until they'd handed the canteen back.

"We were riding stagecoach and got bushwhacked." The preacher spoke for them. "Whoever did it came at us in the night. Bent Feather and his bunch found what was left of us come morning."

"I doubt that. You wouldn't be alive. What makes you think it was Bent Feather?"

"Well, for one thing, the feather. He looked like someone who'd eat your heart out soon as look at you. He left us staked out naked in the sun to die."

"Yet you're here."

"Big fella there was able to pull his stakes loose."

"I can imagine that. Lucky for you."

"We're full of luck today." The preacher managed half a grin that slipped to a frown.

"Well, if you think that was Bent Feather, and you fellas are all watered up, we've got to go. He's the very Comanche we're after. Rustled some cattle and was turning it into jerky by laying it on rocks in the sun on top of Round Bluff until Bentley and his boys run them off."

"What about the stagecoach being robbed? You gonna look into that too?"

"Might as well. Long as we're in the area." Stubbs started to turn his horse.

"Hey, you can't just off and leave us like that!" The preacher's voice rose to a higher pitch.

"Why not?"

"Is your captain Marberry?"

"Yep. How'd you come to know that?"

"Happens I owe him a bucket of poker money. You leave me out here to die and he finds out about it, how you suppose he's gonna feel?"

"Well, blast it." Stubbs thought a moment. "Jenkins!"

One of the men pulled out from the others and came up to Stubbs, leaned on his saddle horn, waiting.

"Pick a detail of three and take these men to town. Ride right back here pronto when you're through. We'll be yonder." He nodded up the road from where Justin and the others had come.

Jenkins called out a couple of names, "Bo Grace. Zed Simmons." Then he turned to Stubbs. "I don't know about the big one there. Doubt he can ride behind anyone unless they're on a Percheron or some such."

Stubbs looked over the rest of his men. "Sully, you let the big fella ride that cavalry mare of yours. You can double with Preston until Jenkins brings yours back."

Justin scrambled up behind Jenkins. Lucas and the preacher each got up behind a rider. Not their favorite way of riding, but a good sight better than walking out here. It took Francis a couple of tries to swing himself up onto the brown mare. He hadn't done much riding.

"I'll tell you one thing, if it's a help to you." The preacher spoke to Stubbs.

"What might that be?"

"It's about the trail of the men who robbed the stage."

"And?"

"One of the horses might be getting ready to throw a shoe. One nail had half come out and was bent over, left a distinctive print."

Stubbs drew his horse closer to where the preacher sat behind a Ranger. "You let us worry about the tracking. You hear? We've got us Irish Mike over there." He nodded toward the oldest of them, a wiry small man with gray hair. "He's done right by us . . . if you don't count the time he said he saw a lot of Injun sign and it turned out to be a herd of mustangs."

Mike turned his head and spat.

"And Bo there with you is as good a tracker as comes along."

"One more thing," the preacher said. "The Injuns took some fresh horse flesh. They'll be stopping someplace soon to cook it."

Stubbs glared at the preacher, but said nothing. He let loose the reins of his horse and gave it his heels. He took off in the beginning of a new whirl of dust. The rest of his men followed him.

They were out of sight by the time Jenkins turned and started off toward town.

Well, Justin had his wish. He bounced along behind his Ranger. He was part of something now. Not particularly daring or exciting, but a whole darned lot better than walking in the sun without water. He glanced back. None of the others were smiling, but they probably felt as glad as he did all the same.

CHAPTER FOUR

As soon as Justin slid off from behind Jenkins, the Ranger reached for the reins Francis held out, turned his horse, and headed back out of town with the other two men behind him. It would probably take them a while to catch up with Stubbs and the rest of the group. Maybe not if they rode hard. Justin looked at the sky. He guessed they'd taken more than a couple of hours to go the eleven or so miles. The horses had still made short work of it . . . compared to walking, and with no water. He imagined they'd be sprawled out there somewhere by now. Lucky. The preacher had said they were lucky. He glanced around at the town.

Jenkins had dropped them off in front of a small, unpainted wooden building where the windows were bars.

"You think we ought to stop in to give the sheriff our story?" Lucas said.

"You can if you want. I'm feeling off balance until I get a six-shooter and ammo," the preacher said. "How about you?"

"I intend to go yonder." Lucas nodded toward the general store across the dirt street.

"Suit yourself." The preacher spun on his heel and started off down the street.

Justin followed Lucas, though he didn't know for sure what was in his father's wallet just yet. Didn't seem wise to be out west in a town where he knew no one went without a sidearm. His dad's had been a good one. He wished some Comanche

40

wasn't riding around with it just now.

"I'll join you later." Francis took off down the street the other way.

When they were halfway across the street Justin glanced that way. A sign said: "Saloon." Plain and simple, and just what Francis would want. His empty flask mattered more to him than being armed. Justin wondered if a dusty old false-front place like that would have the kind of red wine Francis was used to sipping. He doubted it very much.

The streets were wide. You could drive a herd of cattle down the middle, which had probably happened. They were in cattle country. No railroad passed through or nearby, so herds of cattle passing through was what sustained the town—that or the saloon for thirsty cowhands, or the jail, for those who took their fun too far. A few businesses lined either side. He'd seen the blacksmith shop and the livery stable coming into town. He saw a small clothing shop, mostly men's things. Most women made their clothes at home.

Lucas walked through the open front door of the general store. Justin followed him. Inside the store was dim and small; the shelves were stacked high enough a small ladder that leaned inside the door was needed to get to some of the goods. The place was a wonderland. The three of them headed toward a rack by the counter at the back where the store displayed long guns and pistols. They passed a small display of fresh garden produce that looked like it had just been picked, a pretty rare sight.

A woman stood at the back counter talking with a thin balding man in suspenders. "I don't know how you can send your money off to those East-coast places, Mr. Morton, but can't pay me as soon."

"I've told you, Sara. I need their goods in the store."

"You need mine as well. They sell better than your other

goods. Should I set up and sell out of a wagon in town?"

"You're welcome to try. But you know you don't have the time."

The woman sighed, turned, and walked past Lucas and Justin. Her mouth pressed tight on a face that had seen more than one or two dust storms but had still managed to stay pretty, if she could only smile. She passed on out the front door.

Justin stepped up to the back counter. "What's the name of this town? I asked that Ranger, Jenkins, on the way here, but he said he didn't rightly know."

"It's Bentley. But they should call it Brimstone. Almost did, at first. Folks came across a couple of hot springs before they dug wells here. Ben, the saloon owner, said he'd heard of a town called Hot Springs. Besides, the water tasted like the backwaters of hell. So there you have it."

Justin turned back to the pistols that lay in the display. There was a Colt six-shooter like his father's, a little British Webley Bull Dog with a large chip out of its black handle, and a larger Navy revolver he doubted would fit his holster, but might well fit his wallet better. He eased his father's wallet out of his pocket to take a peek inside.

"Just how old are you, son?"

Justin looked up. "Fifteen. Why? Does it matter?"

"Not to me. But I'd rather coin than paper money, and if it's Confederate script you can forget it altogether."

The man's hair was gray to mostly white and big clumps of it stuck out of either oversized ear. His eyes followed Justin's hands as he opened the wallet. Justin turned away so only he could look inside. Empty.

He almost reeled back a step. How were they supposed to get along out west and have their adventure if his father hadn't brought along a single dollar?

Justin turned back to the storekeeper. "Would you like to buy a pretty good holster?" He was going to need some eating money. "And this silver watch? It was my father's."

"That's no kind of silver, son. A buck, for each, and that's stretching it."

"Okay. I guess. You know where I can find a Sara Bolger?"

"If you had a hook you could of caught her a short while back. That was her just a leaving the store." He turned to Lucas. "I guess you've got your eye on the Peacemaker."

"Can you charge it to Bentley?"

"You working for him?"

"Gonna be. He sent for me."

"I suppose." His face grew wily while making a notation in a large cloth-backed journal. "He's bringing a lot of you fellers in. What's he up to? Gonna start the war all over again just 'cause his side lost?"

CHAPTER FIVE

Francis strolled through the saloon's open doorway. It had none of the little swinging doors he'd put on almost every saloon in his dime novels. Just as well. He wove through the dim room and the scattering of unmatched tables on his way to the bar.

An unoccupied bench and upright piano pressed against the far right wall. It didn't have a bullet hole in it, but that's the way he'd paint it when he wrote it up. He always liked to think and wonder about how an object that large got hauled way the devil out here. In the back of some wagon, no doubt. The place inside looked hazy as a half-developed Mathew Brady photograph at this hour and had a smell he couldn't describe. Certainly not just dust, dried sweat, and perhaps dried blood. Something gamier than that, and not in the least pleasant.

Two old gaffers sat in the back nursing glasses of beer that no longer showed any sign of foam. Three men of mixed middle ages sat at a table, mule skinners from their clothes, the sort to work on the freight wagons that supplied the little stores of towns like Bentley. They were a hardworking lot, their clothes and hats still covered in dust. These men, who spent long hours cracking the whip over their mule teams, now pushed pasteboard cards across a warped table and shared a bottle of something that didn't even bear a label. These were the best moments of their long days, spent in a place like this. Dim by midday, though it was sunny outside. Francis shook his head.

A younger cowhand sat by himself in the middle of the bar,

as if taking over the whole of it. Francis supposed women found the man handsome. At the least, he thought so, with his hair slicked back that way, and clean-shaven. Francis reached up to feel the stubble on his own chin. The bartender, who leaned over the counter the cowhand's way, looked up as Francis approached. The two stopped talking as Francis got to the bar to tower over them. He ignored the cowboy, fixed on the saloon keeper. "What's your name?"

"Ben."

"What I want, Ben, is wine. Red wine, if you have such."

"You have got to be joshing." The cowhand knocked back the snifter of bourbon in front of him and reached for the bottle at his elbow.

"No. No, I'm not." Francis leaned across the bar, nearer Ben. "Do you have something good?"

"Well, I have some red and some white."

"What kinds are they?"

"Well, one is the red one, the other isn't."

"You don't have anything in bottles, shipped in from an estate? You know, from France?"

"I have heard it all now," the man seated at the bar said.

Francis held up a right fist the size of a ham. He let Ben see the glittering edge of a gold coin between his fingers.

"Well, I just now recall I have something that might serve. Came with the first shipment of stuff to open and has never had any use before . . . until now. Got it thinking of Captain Bentley. Turns out he's a bourbon man. Sour-mash Kentucky bourbon, at that."

Francis noticed that was what the cowhand was drinking. Pretty pricy stuff for someone riding the dusty end of a herd.

Ben turned and opened a cabinet behind him, dug around, finally pulled out two dusty bottles. Once they stood on the counter he took a bar rag and wiped them off.

Francis picked them up. One eyebrow lifted. He looked at the second bottle, smiled to himself. "How much?"

Ben named a price, one he must have supposed absurd, but wasn't able to suppress a grin.

"I'll give you half of that, which is more than they're worth. But chances are this is as good as I'll come by out in these parts."

"Just where the hell you from? Back east?" The cowhand's voice grew louder.

"Of course I am. Everyone was once. Even you, it's likely."

"Are you calling me a Yankee?"

"I wouldn't do you that honor."

"Take it easy there, Gabe." The bartender turned to Francis. "Okay to the price. Let's see the coin." Ben seemed glad to rid himself of two dusty bottles at a price he could only dream of. He rushed to close his deal before these two got out of hand.

"I'm going to need a corkscrew. And a glass. Let me make sure these are okay."

"What do you mean . . . ?" Gabe started.

"Stow it." Ben turned from Gabe to watch Francis open the bottle, pour a taste into a jigger glass.

He took a sip. "Ah."

Francis dropped the coin he held into the extended hand. Ben reached below the bar, brought up a cigar box, and made change. Francis took out his silver flask and began to carefully fill it.

"Hey, I'm talking to you."

Francis glanced down. Gabe wore his six-shooter slung low on his right hip. So he fancied himself handy and fast with it.

"You hear me?"

Francis could hear and detect something behind the words, more than just a little whiskey, perhaps some leftover raw hate from a war that hadn't gone the way Gabe had hoped. He spoke

46

loud, so every head turned his way. Maybe he was the sort who needed an audience.

While Francis was still jamming the coins into his pocket, Gabe went for his gun.

Gabe had been sitting there sucking down whiskey for who knew how long, and Francis was one devil of a lot faster than anyone gave him credit for. Gabe's hand was still coming up as Francis grabbed the wrist, twisted the gun away, and stood waiting for Gabe's next move.

Ben reached under the bar. Francis looked him in the eye and shook his head. He held Gabe's pistol by its barrel in his left hand, but it would be easy enough to turn and aim. Ben's hands came back empty, and he put them flat onto the bar top. His eyes were open wide and stayed fixed on Francis.

From the corner of his eye Francis saw Gabe's fist coming at him. He had loaded up and put a lot of his weight behind it. When the fist was inches from his face, Francis stepped to the side, lifted Gabe off the floor with one hand and flipped him into a forward roll. He stepped toward him and swung a boot toe that caught Gabe firmly in the seat of the pants and sent him into another circus roll.

Francis had turned back to the bar by the time he heard the scramble as Gabe got to his feet and ran out the open front door.

Ben's hands had stayed put. As the only truly sober person in the room, he had a fair idea of just how fast and strong Francis might be.

Francis placed Gabe's gun on the bar and picked up his two wine bottles. "Good doing business with you, Ben."

Gabe burst back into the saloon, working the lever of the rifle he carried as he came in. "Now we'll see . . ."

It was as far as he got. Someone in black stepped out of the shadows behind him and had a gun up to the back of Gabe's head. The sound of the hammer clicking back sounded loud enough to be the gates of hell opening. "Drop it."

Gabe did. The rifle clattered to the wooden floor.

"Make yourself scarce." The voice came out low and rasping, like metal being torn in half.

Gabe turned, took in the preacher's bit of white on the collar, and the gun that still pointed at his face in an unwavering hand. He headed toward the door in a near trot.

The preacher holstered his gun. Picked up the rifle and put it on the bar beside Gabe's pistol.

"Didn't see you back there in the shadows," Francis said.

"You weren't supposed to." The preacher went to the bar, poured a shot into the glass Gabe had been drinking from. He knocked it back.

"You seem to have armed yourself quickly enough."

The preacher nodded. "I usually do. Where are you off to?"

"Livery, to get a buggy."

"Then where?"

"We'll see."

The preacher shrugged, poured another shot.

"You coming?" Francis asked.

"I just got a hotel room, and I'm off to Madame Fifi's lounge of stimulation."

"Is that really her name?"

"Saves a lot of guesswork."

"Didn't know a town this size would have such a house."

"It's a cattle town. Of course it would."

"Well, enjoy. You're one strange padre, but you had my back, so I owe you one. By the by, what's your name?"

"You can call me Father Abaddon."

"Is that your real name?"

"What do you think?"

CHAPTER SIX

Five minutes later Justin and Lucas stepped back out onto the wooden sidewalk, then onto the dirt street. Lucas was armed again, and Justin had two dollars in his wallet. Should have sold the wallet too, though he doubted he'd get a dime for it. He was still harboring a few dark and questioning thoughts about his father when they heard yelling coming from down the street.

A man came half flying and half stumbling out through the saloon doorway. He hit the end of the sidewalk, just missed a wooden hitching rail, and flipped out onto the street to land on his back. He scrambled to his feet, found his hat, and dusted himself off. He glanced back toward the saloon. The man rushed to his roan horse, grabbed his Winchester out of its saddle sheath and charged back inside.

"Oh, my heavenly stars." The storekeeper stood out in front of the general store with a broom in his hand. "That was Gabe Bentley, as I live and breathe."

"Draw a lot of waters do the Bentleys?" Lucas had loaded his revolver and carried the rest of a box of .44 ammo in his left hand.

"They own half the town. That clothing store yonder, the livery, and, hell, this place."

Barely a minute or two later Gabe came outside at a run. He undid the reins on the roan, hopped on, and took off for the far end of town.

While Justin and Lucas watched, Francis stepped out the

front door with two bottles of wine under his arm. He glanced around, spotted them, and started their way.

"He shouldn't ought to have done that." The storekeeper shook his head, started sweeping.

"I'm wondering just *how* he did it," Lucas said.

"All the same." The storekeeper swept harder.

"What happened in there?" Lucas nodded toward the saloon as Francis came up to them.

"Not much, but it happened all at once."

"What was it about?"

"I don't take mocking, or sass. Man tried to josh me for drinking wine. I didn't stand for it."

"Neither did he. His pants were shining the road there for a minute." Lucas chuckled. "You see where the preacher went?"

"He said he got a room in the hotel. He was going off to Madame Fifi's red-light house after I saw him last."

"I'm starting to wonder just what kind of a preacher he is," Justin said.

"Must want to get a handle on what sin is first hand, I figure." Francis glanced down at Justin. "Didn't you get a gun? I thought that's what you were after."

"He decided to wait, sell his holster instead."

Francis nodded, could guess what that meant. "Where to now?"

"I'm off to the livery to get a horse if I'm to work on the Bentley spread." Lucas tilted his head in the direction the rider on the roan horse had just taken off. "Got some feathers to un-ruffle, no doubt."

"That fellow was a Bentley? No wonder his nose wasn't right." Francis shrugged.

The three of them walked down the street, looking as little like trouble on foot as Justin could imagine if he hadn't just seen some of Francis's handiwork.

As they got closer, Justin could make out some weather-faded letters that had been whitewashed onto the front of the unpainted livery, some of the letters with drip marks running down. The lettering proclaimed: "Sid's Stable."

The livery owner was out front, his back to a saddled sorrel horse. He held its left hind hoof up and had a horseshoe nail in his mouth. With one hand holding the hoof, he yanked a bent nail out with a tool, put the fresh nail in place, and started to hammer it in with the same tool.

"Whose horse is that?" Francis asked as they came up to him.

The man looked up at them, glaring. "What do you want?"

"Are you Sid? And do you have a buggy we could hire for the day?"

"Yep. Yep." He hit the nail one more time and let the horse's foot down, stepping away with the quick care of someone who'd been kicked once or twice before in his life.

Once Sid had Lucas on a saddled horse and headed off toward the Bentley spread, he went inside and came out with a carriage. Went back in and this time led out a bay gelding. He had the tack thrown over one shoulder.

"You know how far out it is to Sara Bolger's place?"

Sid stopped what he was doing and looked up at Francis.

"Who wants to know?"

"I do, and I'm paying in gold coin."

Sid collected his rental fee and stuffed it into a pocket.

"Well, then. She's out thataway, 'bout eleven miles outside the other end of town. You'll see her place far off to the left. Has a fence. You can't miss it."

Francis and Justin stepped away while Sid finished rigging the buggy. Francis leaned his head down close to Justin. "Why don't you let me have a look at that map? I might be willing to buy it off you."

"Nope." Justin saw Sid glance their way, so he spoke in a near whisper. "What makes you think my map is real?"

"Maybe it's not. There are a lot of fakes out there. I should know."

"Still, no."

"Look, kid. You're broke and I'm offering you real money for something you don't know to be worth anything. In gold coin if you want."

"What makes you think it might be real?"

"The paper. I know what kind was used by my publisher to dupe anyone who'd buy."

Justin was spared answering. Sid waved them over to their carriage that was ready to go. Without asking, Francis climbed up and took the reins. There was barely room for Justin to squeeze in beside him.

CHAPTER SEVEN

Jobe Jenkins reined in his horse, Old Top. He sat the gelding while Zed Simmons and Bo Grance rode up to him and stopped. Bo had the lead to the extra horse, Sully's mount, looped over his saddle horn. He'd switched out from reins so he and the horse wouldn't be bumping into each other on the gallop.

"What say we water the horses yonder? There's a piece of creek." Jobe nodded toward the string of cottonwoods and sycamore that marked a stream big enough to support them. "Keep an eye out. Where there's game and water . . ." He didn't need to say the rest. They knew the nature of Indian haunts.

"Won't Stubbs be waiting for us?" Zed bent forward to pat his horse's neck.

"Like as not he's already rode off on one trail or the other, after the redskins or whoever robbed the stagecoach."

They rode across an open rolling field of tall grass, starting to dry light brown in the sun. All of Texas once looked like this, back when the Indians burned off the open fields each year so the buffalo grass could grow. Jobe had ridden over a good part of Texas, but he hadn't seen anything like the great herds of buffalo that once ranged across the area.

He led the way down a slope through a pathway that opened up into a gravel bar that ran along the stream. They watered the horses, then tied them to take their canteens and fill them upstream.

"I'll be." Bo stared up at a limb of an old, long-dead live oak where a row of turkeys roosted. He slipped quietly back to his horse and got his gun. On these short sorties, they didn't always bring along the pack mule. Any chance to get a deer or other game was what kept them fed.

Bo was the right person for the job as well. Jobe had grown up using on old Enfield musket, the kind that was okay for birds when loaded with fine shot, but still kicked enough to be referred to as a gun that got meat on both ends. He'd had many a sore shoulder. When he'd mustered into the Rangers, he'd gotten a standard .50-caliber Sharps carbine and a .45 Colt pistol—not given, since the cost was deducted from his pay. He had since traded the Sharps out for one of the new center-fire .44-caliber Winchester carbines. Most of the sidearms of the others were Colts or Smith & Wesson six-shooters. The long guns the others carried—carbines or rifles—ranged from Sharps, Henrys, to the preferred Winchesters like Jobe's. But Bo, the best shot of them all, thought the Winchester too light and had traded his Sharps in for a .45-70 Springfield sporting rifle. He also carried a couple of rest sticks three feet long, tied together with a leather thong a half foot short of one end. When riding he could use the sticks as a quirt to speed along his horse. To shoot, he used them, long ends down and propping up the barrel of his rifle, with the short ends as a V rest. Very little game got past him, and Jobe had seen him drop a deer from a distance that he wouldn't have even considered trying himself.

Bo stepped on stones getting across to the other bank. He eased closer. Jobe heard three shots. That meant three turkeys. Bo had grown up in East Texas hunting just about every day for the family supper. He could shoot the eyebrows off a gnat at thirty yards.

"Hey, you better come look at this."

"What is it?" Jobe looked across the stream to where Bo had

been gathering up the turkeys and now stood waving him to come over.

Jenkins sighed and picked his way across where wide flat rocks formed a stepping stone path across. On the other side he went out across a deer path that ran parallel to the stream. He bent down to the tracks that had attracted Bo's attention.

"Yep. Sounds like what that preacher was talking about. Horse may be getting ready to throw a shoe. Bent nail on one hoof, just like that preacher said."

"Looks like there were three of them."

"Well, if Stubbs is off following the redskins, let's see if we can find out anything about these three jaspers. They seem to be taking the back way to town."

They hurried back to their horses to mount up.

Four hours later, when Jobe and the others caught up with Stubbs, he and the other Ranger men were gathered around a burned-out fire at what had been Bent Feather's camp. While tying up his horse, Jobe could see that the Indians had built three fires to cook both sides of the horse ribs. They'd picked the bones clean. They'd also hacked some mesquite bushes partially down and they'd cut the rest of the horse meat into thin strips and draped it on a finely built scaffold to cook it over a low fire for carrying.

"Why didn't you take off after them?" Jobe asked Stubbs.

"Well, I figure they've had a bite, but heard us coming and lit out before their carrying meat was done cooking. They'll be riding like a brush fire just now. We'll give them time to think they're clear of us. When their guard is down we'll sneak up on them. Besides, the boys tied up their horses in a bed of rattlesnakes, and we've got two bit horses, one with a head the size of a barrel and the other bitten on the front leg just above the ankle and swollen up to his body. Neither's able to walk right yet, and we were a horse short anyway. What took you fellas so long?"

Stubbs held a strip of the meat and took a bite from one end. He chewed, and frowned. Before Jobe could answer, the sergeant said, "You got any salt? The meat's hardly fit to eat this way."

Jobe nodded back to where the two men with him had tied up. "Bo shot three turkeys back there. No salt, but they're tolerable good without."

"Better get them cooking. We've got time before the horses are all fit to go."

Once Jobe had the men busy pulling feathers and putting more wood on the fire, Stubbs said, "Now we have time."

"We were coming back and when we went to water the horses, and give Bo a chance at those turkeys . . ."

"It's no chance when Bo's shooting."

Jobe ignored the interruption. "We came across the tracks of three horses riding along on the other side of the creek, taking the back way to town. One of them had the bent horseshoe nail that preacher fella mentioned."

"Like that fella was a preacher."

"Anyways, we followed the trail all the way to the back end of town before the tracks got mixed in and walked over. We got slowed down here and there. There's cattle running loose all through here, and we had to circle around a few times to make sure we stayed on the trail. It helped we'd guessed where they were heading."

"Any idea who they were?"

"None just yet. Just three guys."

Stubbs held out the strip of meat in his hand, offering it to Jobe. Hot fat dripped off one end. Jobe shook his head. He'd wait on the turkeys. Stubbs took another bite, frowned, but chewed. "You know, won't be long before no one will be sending money and letters by stagecoach no more. The railroads will take over that, and be safer. Someone must've had a payroll coming in to somewhere."

"And someone had to know about it. Someone from Bentley."

Stubbs nodded. "We get a chance after we're done with Bent Feather, we might could ride into Bentley and find out what we can. Be a chance to eat something better than dead horse anyways."

He tossed the piece he held into the fire they'd started and went over to get his canteen. The flames leaped up in welcome to embrace the meat's oils.

CHAPTER EIGHT

"I told you that you didn't have to bring me out here."

"Sure. You could have walked." Francis waved a hand behind them. "You'd still be back there plodding away in the sun."

The wind swept across Justin's face, tugging at his hair. They'd maintained a pretty good pace, the horse in a trot most of the way.

They were about to the place in the road where the livery-man had said they ought to start looking for Sara Bolger's place, and Justin was straining his eyes to the left, when he heard shots being fired. A couple of quick shots, then two slow and steady ones back.

"Now what the devil?" Francis muttered. He snapped the reins and picked up the pace heading that way.

Justin thought about the empty holster he'd had to sell and the tiny derringer that was all Francis carried. They sure seemed to be heading hell-for-leather toward more trouble than they could handle. Justin's first thought at hearing gunshots was to head the other direction. Not crazy man Francis, who'd rented the buggy.

The buggy spun its wheels as it left the road and turned up the lane in a spray of gravel. As it tilted to the left and right, Justin was thrown around, first slamming into Francis, next nearly flying off into the air to his right. He clung to the wooden seat with his left hand and the rail with his right. The horse ran at full gallop, and as the buggy hit bumps, Justin bounced up and down, not sure if the cart would hold together through all this.

Ahead he saw a puff of smoke from a window of the house, heard the shot. An Indian carrying a goat came running up the lane toward them, looked up, saw them, and dropped the goat. He veered off to his right, Justin's left. Another Indian sat his horse and held another horse, waiting. The running Indian hopped onto his horse from behind and the two took off, from standing still to full gallop in a heartbeat.

Justin saw that the Indian who had been holding the other's horse wore a burgundy jacket that hung large and loose on him.

"Would you look at that? The cheeky bastard." Francis fumbled to get his tiny derringer out. A fat lot of good it would do. The two Indians were almost out of sight, even though the land was flat where they rode. Now that the buggy had drawn to a stop just short of where the goat lay, Justin decided they were either two of the Comanche bunch that had staked him out earlier, or looked just like them.

"Fetch that goat, would you?"

"You sure?" Justin hesitated to climb down from the buggy.

Francis nodded.

Justin got down and went to the goat, a white one with large black spots and short horns. Its throat had been slit. Blood still covered the neck, though it had begun to dry at the edges. He looked up at Francis.

"Just get it. That goat's not going to bite you. Best not leave it out here for those Comanche or any other critters."

He climbed back onto the buggy, held the goat on his lap, the neck side out in case the jostling ride made it bleed more.

They took a slower pace getting up to the ranch house, which looked odd to Justin's eye. The house appeared to be made of thick abode, more fortress than pueblo. Instead of windows, it had narrow slits, and a long gun barrel poked out of one of them. As they came up to the front closed door, a small blonde woman stepped around the side of the house and pointed a Winchester at them. "What's your business here?"

It was a mighty stern voice for a woman who couldn't weigh a hundred pounds, stood no more than five feet tall, and still wore an apron with dabs of flour on it. Aside from a line here and there on her face, ones that more likely came from laughing than frowning, she could be mistaken for someone in her teens. Still, she could look serious as an injured badger when the moment called for it, as did this one.

"Are you Sara Bolger?" Justin's voice quavered, not used to looking down the barrel of a gun, one that recently had been fired.

"Who are you?"

"I'm Justin Bodean. Your nephew, I think."

"Where's Cletus?"

"I'm afraid we buried him, ma'am." Francis took off his hat.

"Why? Was he dead?"

Francis started to grin, suppressed it. "Our stagecoach got jumped a ways on the other side of town. He took a bullet."

"Didn't have the sense to duck?"

"Wasn't much ducking going on. Happened at night."

"Well, you'd best come in, then. I'll make coffee and you can tell me about it."

The front door opened and a small boy, no more than eleven or so, stood in the doorway, holding a long muzzle loader that towered over him. That had been the barrel sticking out of the window.

"Scamp. You'd best dress out that goat. Justin here can help you."

The boy put his gun back inside and came out to them. He wore homespun yellow-brown pants and a shirt, once white, that might have been homemade as well.

Justin didn't know how much help he'd be at dressing out a goat. He'd never so much as cleaned a fish or dressed out a chicken. Yet he handed the goat down to Scamp and followed him around to the back of the house.

A wooden ladder, made of limbs with the bark still on, led from the roof. Someone was climbing down from it, carrying a double-barreled shotgun that looked heavy and made it hard for the person to hold onto the ladder.

At the bottom, the figure turned around. Justin took in the red of hair pulled tight back and covered by a blue bandanna, a smudge of dirt or gunpowder on one check and a smeared line of it across the forehead of a girl. A girl. One who looked to be Justin's age. She wore blue coveralls over a fading red shirt.

"Oh, my stars." She whirled and ran inside.

He turned to Scamp, who was sharpening a knife. "Who was that?"

"Just Button."

"Your sister."

"Kind of." Scamp lifted the goat up onto the flat of a stump that served as his table. He started to slit open its belly. Justin looked away.

"What do you mean, 'kind of'? Is she your sister or not?"

"You mean your cousin, don't you?" Scamp held back the beginning of a grin that was slowly slipping through anyway.

"Let's just clean this dern goat." Justin forced himself to take a step closer and watch how it was done.

Justin carried a pan of the freshly cut meat inside. The house smelled good. He saw a wide fireplace and large black pot hanging over one side of the fire. A coffeepot rested in the embers on the other side. Francis sat at a wooden table that served for the meals. Even then, as a man who stood six-foot-six, he was taller sitting down than Justin's aunt Sara was standing. A small blonde girl hovered near Francis, looking up at him as if he was the eighth wonder of the world, and to her maybe he was.

"Missy, say hello to your cousin, Justin. Then come help me with the stew. It was going to be a vegetable one. But since them Comanche saw fit to kill a goat, we might as well enjoy the fruits of their labor. Wouldn't get any money trying to sell goat meat in town just now anyways."

The little girl gave Justin a timid wave, then shot over to stand beside her mother. There was no questioning the relationship here. She looked just like her mom, a miniature and younger version.

"So, Mister Francis Marion Gallagher, how is it you happen to know Justin and did him the kindness to fetch him out to my place?"

Justin glanced toward Francis, who seemed more at home here than he felt himself yet. He had seemed damned all interested in that map. Justin had wondered before about the big man's motives. All he knew was what Francis had told him, and Justin hadn't been long in the west, but it seemed a right generous place for people to make up whatever they wanted about themselves and who they really were.

Justin said, "he was on the stagecoach with us, helped me bury Dad. We went through some things together. Endured them, so to speak." Justin could see them again, all naked and tied out in the sun, waiting to die. He chose not to include that in his narrative. "His publisher sent him out west to gather flavor for books he writes, so it doesn't matter where he goes, as long as whatever happens is interesting to him."

"How come I've never heard of you?"

"Have you ever heard of Tornado Trey Calvin?" Francis said.

"Is he some sort of outlaw? We've got those out here by the bushel full."

"He's the character I write about as Ben Blunt in dime novel

62

adventures."

"Can you make a living at that?"

"As long as I don't run out of colorful characters."

"I imagine you'll run out of notebooks before you get written all the interesting people you'll find out in these parts." Sara chuckled.

"Sara here was just telling me how this place used to be Fort McCord, one of the smaller pueblo forts along the western frontier." Francis swept a wide hand at the thick walls that surrounded them. "During the Civil War, the Union troops were pulled out of places like this. Sara and her husband moved in, claimed a homestead, and their claim was honored."

"Until Luther died. Fever." Sara was dropping the chunks of meat into the pot while the tiny Missy had all she could do to stir the big wooden handle of a spoon. Still, she seemed to enjoy the task. Probably made her feel part of keeping the household going and together.

Justin had noticed Scamp hadn't dragged his feet either when it came to chores, but had leaped right to them.

"I will say, I don't know when I've seen a bigger hearth in a smaller place," Francis said. "In a place like this it's the whole of your kitchen and center of your parlor too."

"Justin's uncle Roger helped build it when he was staying here. He was the handy one with tools. Built all the wooden furniture, and put in the hearth. Luther helped. But Roger was the skilled craftsman."

"Did he die of the fever too?"

"No. He left just before any of the little ones were born. He traipsed off to seek his fortune, and Luther never heard from him again. Shame, too. He'd have always been welcome back."

"Why? Were you needing a barn built?"

Sara chuckled. "No. But he did help build a root cellar and the small outbuilding where we keep the feed for the goats and what tools we use to keep the garden growing."

Justin glanced around inside. It seemed small, too small to be called cozy. He could see where bedrolls had been rolled up and lined one wall. On the far side, a calico sheet hung across one corner, giving that bed some privacy. Probably Aunt Sara's.

He was about to ask the question when the calico drape was pulled to the side from behind and Button emerged, looking quite different from the way Justin had seen her a few moments ago. Her long hair was loose and brushed back to fall red and straight halfway down her back. She'd wiped the smudges off her face and she wore a dress, one made of the same material as the drape.

"Well, dip me in gravy and spin me over the fire. I do believe you're blushing, Justin." Francis leaned back in his chair and laughed. The chair, like the table, was sturdy and handcrafted, in the manner of the ladder Justin had seen outside.

"Oh, for heaven's sake. How are you going to help me cook dressed like it was Sunday?"

"I'll manage." Button blushed too.

Button went over to take the spoon handle from Missy.

"But the homestead wasn't going to hold up when Luther died. There has to be a man as head of household."

"How did you get around that, Sara?" Francis leaned forward, his thick forearms resting on the table.

"A neighbor, Mildred Riley, watched the children. She was Button's mother, before the fever took her as well. I lost two children to the fever too. I used what little we had set aside to go all the way east to Washington, D.C. The only way around it was for me to get a patent for the idea of a woman taking over a homestead claim. So that's what I done."

"Can you imagine that, Justin? There is indeed some spunk and grit in your family line."

Francis's words reminded Justin of his father. He wouldn't

have called him very gritty. Himself either, come to that. Back when those Comanche had ridden up to them, his first thought had been to climb under what was left of the stagecoach and hide.

"How come your name's Bolger?"

"I went back to my maiden name for the legal papers. It's not that different from Bodean. Don't matter much what people call me, as long as I know who I am. Tell you the truth, I wasn't too sad about not being a Bodean no more. Sorry if that stings, Justin. But those Bodean men. *Hmpf.* The kids are all Bodeans, except Button. She's a Riley."

Justin noticed Button sneaking peeks at him as she stirred the stew. For the first time he began to wonder how he'd hold up now if in the same circumstance. Different, or would he be the same coward his father had proven himself to be?

"Well, I must say, you have certainly made a home out here in the wilderness." Francis looked around the small room.

"If you don't count having to fend off Indians and every other sort of thing, and they're not the worst of it."

"Have you had many of these brushes with the Comanche?"

Scamp came inside in time to hear. He said, "Bent Feather himself was right outside the front door. Mom shot his horse out from under him and told him to git."

"So it's not all the easy life out here, then?" Francis held back a chuckle, but not all the way.

"Are you joshing me? If it's not the Comanche it's the coyotes, or snakes, or worse, the Bentleys." Sara set the pan aside and took the spoon handle from Button. She grew agitated and took it out on the stew. "Old man Bentley—Captain Samuel Q. Bentley everyone around here calls him since he came back from serving General Lee—and his two sons, Gabe and Esau, have been pestering us for the past few years. They've tried about everything to get us off this little patch of land."

"Is it water rights? I heard he has cattle," Francis said.

"No. It's just plain meanness. All we do is raise some crop vegetables and the goats, for meat, milk, and cheese. We trade others for what we need, but Captain Bentley has the town folk freezing us out for what they owe us. He owns half the town, from the livery stable to the general store. We have only a few friends and those who still dare to come buy or trade for what we raise. He can line up plenty of people against us."

"Seems like you're holding your own well enough."

"Not like it might seem. It's the taxes that are gonna get us. Time we get feed, seeds, and ammo, we've used up about all we have, and Bentley is squeezing to keep us from getting what else we can. If we can't pay the taxes, we'll lose this land, and right now we're getting close to that. Real close."

CHAPTER NINE

Jobe Jenkins rode out in front on the scout, with Bo Grance beside him. The other Rangers trailed along behind as they followed Bent Feather's trail.

"Blamed if they aren't headed right past the town of Bentley on the other side of the road from what the stage robbers took." Jobe glanced back to Stubbs.

"We'd have probably caught up with them by now if we hadn't needed to wait until all the horses were fit to ride." Stubbs turned his horse to sweep out wide on either side to see that they hadn't missed anything.

Jobe rode up closer to Bo and spoke in a low voice. "That and these pesky redskins doing all they can, by accident or on purpose, to take their trail across every stretch of flat rock that leaves no trail or mixing it in with every herd of cattle they can."

"Oh, I can untangle most of that, given time to sort it out," Bo said. "It's the sarge, whipping us to do it all faster like there's a house afire somewhere, that's making me take guesses now and then. Makes me half as crazy as these Injuns must be."

"That's because you're not wanting to be a captain of the Rangers someday. Stubbs back there is all in a lather to go places. That's why we're chasing redskins just now instead of hugging the trail of whoever robbed that stage."

"Why's that matter a whoop?"

"Well, the captain was a first-rate Indian fighter once. You ever turn your mind to that?"

High on the only nearby mesa, Bent Feather stood to the side of a weathered mesquite trunk and watched the Rangers ride by, their heads down on a trail he'd left for them. Once they were past, he eased back to where the others sat their horses. He waved a hand in the other direction and took off toward where the Rangers had been.

Two or three miles more, and Jobe watched the Comanche sign disappear beneath the hoof marks of a herd of cattle. He glanced over to Bo, who shook his head.

"I'll try riding ahead, see if I can find the tracks on the other side."

Jobe gave Old Top a nudge with his heels. It soon became clear he was going to be hard-pressed to find any sign. It looked to him like someone had run a herd along the trail on purpose to rub out the Indian sign. Who would do that? He thought the path had been leading them toward Sara Bolger's small spread. The Indians would be needing meat again. They'd had nothing since the horse ribs, and the jerky they'd been preparing that had gone to the Rangers.

Jobe sat his horse and waited for the rest of the Rangers to catch up to him.

When they did, he had a short powwow with Stubbs. Then they headed toward the Bolger spread. No one called it the Bodean spread anymore since Luther had died a while back.

Whoever had driven the cattle through had done a right good job of rubbing out any more Indian sign. There was nothing but the marks of horseshoes and cattle hooves. Jobe leaned bent over, half off his saddle when he heard the sound of hooves coming his way.

The rest of the Rangers came up behind him at the same time as those riding the other way rode up and pulled their horses to a halt. Sergeant Stubbs came up to the front.

Facing them were the Bentleys—Captain Samuel Q. Bentley, and his sons Gabe and Esau. Four of his hands rode with him, all of them armed and able to shoot, the only kind of hand Bentley would hire.

Jobe recognized one of the hands. He looked to Stubbs.

"Why, Lucas Brent. Looks like you found a job pretty handy."

"It's what I came to do, work for the Bentley spread."

"You must be pretty handy with a six-shooter, then."

"I get by."

"You have any business, you take it up with me. You hear?" Captain Bentley wore a thick white mustache. His hat and pants were Confederate issue, in case anyone had any doubts about his leaning in the recent disturbance between the states. "Don't be cozying up with my hands. You have any talking to do, you do it to me." His voice stayed gruff, snappish.

"Right now, Mister Bentley . . ."

"Captain Bentley."

"The war's over. Get over it." Stubbs sat up straighter in his saddle, a posture that showed he'd spent plenty of time in the cavalry. "Right now you're obstructing Texas Rangers from doing their job, which at the moment is pursuing a small renegade band of Comanche."

"We'll take care of any Injun killing needs done around here."

"That's not your decision to make. It's ours."

"Why aren't you after whoever robbed that stage line? They made off with my payroll."

Jobe Jenkins had been watching Lucas, who stared in stony silence. But he noticed the two sons, Gabe and Esau, caught each other's eye.

"Now, lest you want to further impede us, I suggest you get

out of our way."

"We're just fetching back our cattle that strayed over onto that damned Kenedy's spread. If we don't, he's apt to brand them as his own . . . when he isn't stealing horses."

"He speaks as highly of you. Now get out of our way."

Bentley sat and frowned at Stubbs. He neither moved his horse nor told his men to move theirs.

Stubbs gave it a moment, then waved an arm. He led the Rangers out and around Bentley and his men.

Once on the other side they picked up to a trot. Jobe thought he heard Stubbs muttering, "Stubborn old cuss."

He had to agree. The old man was every bit of that.

Stubbs glanced at the sky. "Shoulda brought a pack mule if I'd known we'd be out on patrol this long. It's fetching to get dark. We'll bivouac for now, and pick up the trail in the morning. We have anything to eat besides horse meat?"

Zed Simmons glanced to the packs he carried. "We've got beans."

"Damn all beans," Stubbs snapped.

"We could always harvest a calf. Bentley would lay it off in the redskins," Bo said. "He wouldn't know the difference."

"But I would," Stubbs said. "We'll eat beans."

CHAPTER TEN

Through the gun slot windows of the former fort, Justin could see the sky outside fading to gray. Button went around closing the wooden hatches on each window. Just the light of the fire lit the room. Sara hovered by the hearth, a big one that took up a third of one wall of the structure, made smaller because the walls were so thick. That made it seem cozy and safe, and the smell of the stew filled the room to its corners.

Justin stepped closer to his aunt Sara. "There doesn't look to be much room to sleep. Though, tell the truth, I'm more interested in that stew that's cooking. It smells mighty good."

"How long's it been since you've eaten?"

"I was just trying to remember. Two days ago?"

"Oh, my." Sara stirred the stew harder, as if that might speed it up.

Francis sat at the wooden table, the chair beneath him solid enough to hold him, but creaking from the effort. He pulled the cork from the bottle of wine he'd opened at the saloon. "Do you fancy a nip?" he asked Sara.

She shook her head.

He stood and walked over to a wooden shelf that held dishes—plates, bowls, a few tin mugs, and one stemmed glass that looked to be cut crystal. His thick hand settled around it. He swooped it up.

"I'd rather you didn't use that," Sara said. "It's the only surviving one of the two Luther and I drank from on our wedding night."

"It'll be fine. I'll treat it like a son." Francis sat back down at the table and filled the glass with wine.

Sara frowned, glanced at Justin.

He shrugged, stepped closer.

"Just how did this man come to be attached to you like a barnacle?" she whispered.

"I'll tell you later," he whispered back.

Once the adults were around the table—Scamp and Missy happy for the occasion to set their plates on the wide hearth to eat—Francis gave some indication of how he came by his size, emptying two bowls of stew and going back for a third. Sara and Justin glanced to each other.

The wine didn't last the meal, and Francis's voice grew louder. "Don't let me dominate the conversation," he said in a rare moment of insight. "Why don't you tell us what's worrying you, Sara? I can tell it's something."

She glanced to Justin, then the kids, not comfortable with speaking in front of all of them.

"I told you about the taxes. That's part of it. The homestead here is in a precarious spot. I've got Captain Bentley and his spread pressing up against one side of me, and James Kenedy's spread on the other side. Both would as soon gobble up my tiny piece of land. They don't like the fences I've got around the corral and garden."

"And that Esau Bentley has eyes for Button," Scamp said.

"Doesn't either." Button peeked at Justin from her lowered head as she started to gather up the dishes.

"The Bentleys and Kenedys feud and spat with each other all the time, and neither one does a dern thing about the Indians around here. Well, they hobby at it, for fun, but I still lose a goat every now and again."

"You should get a burro. I'm told they defend goats and

sheep," Francis said.

"And buy it with what? Did you know the Bentleys own the livery?"

"Oh." Francis glanced around, taking the measure of the limited interior. "It's going to be crowdy in here for sleeping." He seemed to be winding down after the wine.

"You three—Justin, Scamp and you, Mister Francis—get to camp out in the loft of the goat shed. It's where Scamp sleeps. That's gonna be crowded too. You'll have to get along."

"We'll be fine," Justin said.

"Funny thing," Francis said. He leaned back in his chair, far too comfortable for his own good, Justin thought. "That Lucas told Justin here that he wouldn't have any better chance of surviving than a three-legged horse."

"That's just silly," Button said. "Horse that way couldn't get by at all."

Francis grinned, the silly grin of a man riding a wine horse in his head. He tilted back his head and began to sing in a loud, booming voice, apparently making up the words as he went along.

> *Out on the prairie when the moonlight has friz*
> *You get lost in the stars though you know where you*
> > *is*
> *Nights cold as harsh thunder, days hotter'n hell*
> *Saddle time spent till that chuck wagon bell.*
>
> *Adventure, they said, was out here to be had*
> *In them fool's-gold-rich rocks, where you buried your*
> > *dad*
> *Your ma took an arrow the second day out*
> *Not a person you knew ever died from the gout.*
>
> *Took to cowhandin' for a warm bit of bait*
> *Beans were so tough that they stuck to the plate*

Coffee's so strong it can stand its own guard
Watch out for the man who you think is your pard.

Shoot straight if you must, shoot fast if you can
Tend your own back if you'd grow to a man
Lucky at cards isn't lucky at love
When another man thinks she is his fallen dove.

Rode out of Salinas on a three-legged horse
Hard to say which of you's shot up the worse
A posse behind and Comanches ahead
A flat piece of rock may well be your last bed.

"Oh, my stars," Sara said. "You'll be giving the kids all kinds of fantods and bad dreams now, won't you."

Francis held up a finger that he wasn't finished. He kept going, loud enough to rattle the plates Button held in her milky-white hands, as if frozen in place.

The cattle are fickle, the coyotes bold
Under the moon in a blanket of cold
Sing to the herd as the flames flicker low
The days sure go fast, but the nights are so slow.

Out on the prairie when the moonlight has friz
You get lost in the stars though you know where you
   is
Nights cold as harsh thunder, days hotter'n hell
Saddle time spent till that chuck wagon bell.

Francis stopped at last and the inside of the pueblo fort fell silent enough they could hear the wind outside scraping at the outer walls. He stared at his empty wine glass, picked it up with fingers that showed a slight tremor.

"Scamp, why don't you take Mister Francis outside and show him where you fellas are gonna sleep."

"Won't be a bit of bother at all, ma'am." Francis stood, still holding the empty wineglass. His fingers went slack and the glass fell to the stone floor, shattered into tiny pieces. He glanced down, nearly laughed out loud until he saw Sara's expression. He lowered his oversized head and let Scamp lead him out the door.

As soon as they were out the door, she said, "Now, Missy, you go get yourself ready for bed."

Missy rose and went behind the curtain, the only bit of privacy in the room.

Button finished gathering the dishes, put them into a washtub to deal with later. She got out the broom and started sweeping up the broken glass on the floor.

"Last heirloom I had in the house." Sara sighed.

"I don't know if he knows how awkward and clumsy he is when he's that way."

"You're probably right. But it don't make it right. We were always too poor for Luther to take to drink."

Justin nodded.

Sara leaned closer, kept her voice down. "Now tell me how this man came to be attached to you so. And why?"

"I thought it might be just an act of kindness at first. But I suppose it's the map."

"What map?"

"It's one Uncle Roger sent to my dad. It's a treasure map."

"To what? How would Roger know about any kind of treasure?"

"I'm not sure. He told dad, but he only hinted to me that it was some kind of lost Civil War gold."

"He was in the big disturbance, but as a Union quartermaster. How would he know anything about any gold? He had to go

75

back north with the others. Luther and I stayed behind. Bentley and the others still think of us as Yankees, as a consequence."

"That's all I know."

"Let me have a look at it."

Justin fished the map out of his pocket, slid it across the table to her.

"Well, isn't that a fine kettle of fish."

"You know where the treasure is?"

"Of course not. This map's useless to anyone who doesn't know what the landmarks mean. It could be right around here, but I don't get around that much, except to town and back. To follow this, a person would have to be from around here and familiar with the area. That's if it's even showing the area around here. Even if it is, I couldn't parse out where to look."

"So the map is useless?"

"To you and me anyway."

The night air enveloped Justin, felt cooler, but not enough to keep him awake now that he finally had a meal in his belly. He picked his way through the yard in back of the house and along the goat corral fence until he came to the low shed where he could see a low loft over the stored feed. Scamp was tugging at the end of a blanket.

"There. Got it free." He held it up.

"What are you doing?"

"That lummox has sprawled himself in there and is taking up the whole thing. It would've been crowded anyway. But look at him."

Justin could see Francis on his back, already snoring, with one hand up, where he had been grasping the only blanket, now clutching air.

"Here." Scamp held out the blanket to Justin. "I'll use a horse blanket. We might as well camp on the ground. No sense trying to squeeze in there."

"I'm sorry about him."

"No bother. If it was raining we'd drag him out. But we'll be fine."

Justin spread his blanket, eased down onto it, and lay on his back looking at the stars and crescent moon.

"Do you think your mom is going to be able to make it?"

"Hum?" Scamp's voice sounded groggy. He'd been half asleep as soon as he lay down. "Oh, I guess."

"What makes you think that?"

"She always has before. A lot of folks have come at us and tried to rattle us out of here, but here we are."

"Here you are indeed." Justin heard the beginning of Scamp's snore.

In the far distance a coyote began to howl. For part of a moment Justin didn't think he'd ever fall asleep. Then he did.

CHAPTER ELEVEN

Lucas had his horse saddled while the others were still stirring from their blankets.

"Where do you think you're going?" Captain Bentley sat his horse outside the stirring remuda inside the corral. He stared down at Lucas.

"I think you have an idea." Lucas pulled himself up into the saddle so they were eye to eye.

"It's about the money, isn't it?"

"It's about the money."

"You don't hear the others bellyaching."

"Fine. You've got them, then."

"But you're supposed to be the fastest around. Hell, I paid for your coach here. I paid for your gun, I'm told, as well as the horse you're riding."

"I had some losses too, when that stage got robbed."

"You know the money I was to pay you with was on that stage. I've wired for more from my bank."

"Why not use a local bank?"

"You've seen this town."

"It bears your name."

"Well, the bank doesn't. It belongs to that damned Yankee Kenedy. It's no place to keep any kind of serious money safe. He owns the hotel as well, while I have the saloon and the livery."

Lucas shrugged, rode up to the gate to let himself out.

"I'm damned if I'll let you ride off owing me for a gun and a horse. I'll have you hung as a horse thief."

"Who's gonna hunt me down? Those two sons of yours?"

Bentley gave the matter more thought than it deserved. It was clear to Lucas that the man was playing with no hole card.

"Look, give it today. I've someone I might get some ready cash from. Probably won't cost you a single bullet. The sheriff is going along."

"The sheriff?" Lucas let out a hard huff of wind. "Sheriff Rufus Frazier. "We all know he's had his days. Was a fair to middling gunslinger once, but those days have galloped past him. He's on a downhill slide."

"That's why you're here. He's the authority. You're the enforcement."

"I'd ask why you don't use your boys for that, but I've a guess how capable they are. Maybe for shooting someone in the back."

"You know I don't have to take that from someone like you."

"No. No, you don't, because I'm riding out of here."

Lucas could see the color shoot up the sides of Bentley's neck. He wasn't used to being talked to this way. He'd bossed a lot of men around not long past. But he hadn't ridden with Quantrill either. In the short time he'd been around Bentley, Lucas had figured him for a man used to getting his own way, probably buying his Confederate officer's commission, bossing his men then, and riding his sons hard once he was back on his home spread. It must have slapped him like a branding iron to find a man like Kenedy, from Massachusetts, had gobbled up a big chunk of land next to his spread, as well as half the main businesses in the town.

Bentley spoke through clenched teeth. "Just give it today. If I can't get more money by the next stage, I should be able to squeeze something today."

★ ★ ★ ★ ★

On the ride over to Sara Bolger's tiny spread, nestled between the far edge of Bentley's land and the Kenedy spread, Lucas Brent looked over those riding behind Bentley. There were the two sons, Gabe and Esau, neither one worth a hoot down an empty well as far as he could tell so far. Three other fellas he only knew by nod so far, who had come in with guns worn low and looking more eager for a scrap than to do any cowhand work. Just as well. Roundup was a ways off, unless you were making the sort of midnight runs the two boys were up to with running irons in their kits.

It's not an impossible thing to change a Rocking K brand into a Circle B, but the boys were sloppy enough that about any tomfool could see through the change. That probably didn't matter much, since the other man riding with them was Sheriff Rufus Frazier himself.

He'd taken one look at Lucas and just shaken his head. He might be old enough to have helped Noah count the animals by twos, but there was nothing wrong with his thinking noggin. Behind that long white mustache and tightly pressed mouth was the head of a man who had seen much and said little. Bentley had known what he was doing by rounding the man up and ramrodding him in as sheriff, long before Kenedy had been around.

He watched Bentley, who hadn't looked his way once. For that matter, he hadn't glanced toward either of his sons. He glared straight ahead and rode his Kentucky Walker. Lucas caught the sheriff glancing his way a few times, like he was watching a short fuse burning.

Esau rode up on point, looking for Injun sign, he'd said, but Lucas doubted he was half the scout a Tonk would have been if they'd had one along. They came up to him sitting his horse just outside the Bolger tiny spread, a mere 320 acres, with only part of it, ten acres or so, fenced off for goats and garden, from what Lucas could see. The few horses were corralled with the goats. He spotted the livery buggy Francis had rented. It sat pulled up beside the small feed shed.

The place looked like it had been a fort once. Same sort as where the redskins and buffalo hunters had mixed it up in that fracas north of the Canadian. He hadn't been in on the fray, but he'd heard plenty and ridden past the place once. You get inside a place like that, it's hard to pry you out, especially if you have food and water.

A small boy spotted them and went running inside, yelling something.

People came pouring out of the house. Lucas recognized Francis, and the much smaller Justin, who eased to one side until he stood half behind Francis. One figure came out carrying a double-barrel shotgun, slipped around to the back of the house, then appeared on the roof, with the barrels pointed their way. Another muzzle-loader barrel poked out one of the window slots of the old fort. Then a petite blonde woman, not even as tall as Justin, came out of the house. She stood at the front of the group, held a Winchester low and ready, as if she knew how to use it.

She waited until the group rode up and stopped a dozen feet away. "What is it you want?"

"Your taxes are due, Sara. Overdue. We've come to collect." Bentley's horse took a side step as he shouted.

"You're not the law. Isn't that your puppet sheriff there with you? What's wrong with his tongue?"

"True enough. You are behind in your taxes." The sheriff's voice sounded raspy and stale, little used.

"As are the taxes of others." Sara worked the lever of the rifle. "What is it you want?"

"We have the right to take the land and put it up for bid at a sheriff's sale. You know that."

"As you've done with most the other small pieces. Bentley there and his evil twin Kenedy have been there to gobble them up."

"Don't you call that Yankee any relative of mine!" Bentley's voice could boom when his dander was up.

The person on top on the fort stood and yelled something to Sara.

"Then why's he riding up yonder with his band of scalawags?" Sara hollered.

Around the far corner of Sara's fences, a dozen men came riding their way. Not fast, just full of purpose.

Lucas glanced up to the figure on top of the fort. It was a woman. He could tell that now. A young one. Daughter maybe. Yet she held that gun like she knew how to use it.

As he panned back, Lucas took in Esau, who, unlike the others, didn't stare at the approaching men. He stayed fixed on the young girl on the fort's top. In the short time he'd been around, he'd heard enough about the two Bentley boys to know that Gabe was the one who fancied himself good at cards, but wasn't. Esau, though, had a thing for girls. Young girls. Both boys were snakes, hardly worth a bullet. But the stories he'd heard about Esau were the kind that would have gotten him ridden out of any other town where his father didn't draw as much water as he did. Liked his girls young, way too young. Old man Bentley must've had his hands full bailing those two out time and again. Could be part of why he'd bought himself a sheriff.

Lucas counted the men with Kenedy as they rode up. Three more than in Bentley's group, and the steeds were finer as well. The man might be from up north but, damn, he knew horses. He swept the group, all slingers like Bentley's new hands, froze when he came to the one on the end. The preacher, the one Lucas had seen reloading after the stage shoot-up.

"I'll be blasted," the sheriff muttered. It took a lot for him to break into speech. "You know that one on the end?"

Bentley shook his head.

"Hell, it's a guy named Vin Thomas. He's better known as the Vinegar Kid."

"You don't say."

"Someone called him Vinnie once."

"That happen a lot?"

"Just the one time."

Lucas knew Kenedy owned the hotel in town. Must have been why the preacher had booked a room there. Sure enough, he'd come to town for the same reason as Lucas, but to work for someone else. The preacher, or The Kid, rather, wore his gun lower now, had the predator eyes of someone sizing up the group, already deciding who to take out first. Lucas saw Gabe squirm in his saddle, and Esau back up his horse. The old man was made of tougher stuff. He stared at the Kenedy bunch like they were so many vermin.

"We're here on official tax business. What do you want?" Bentley snapped.

"Good to know. Might want to buy the place at the sheriff's sale, if he announces it this time." Kenedy wore a white hat that matched his white pork chop sideburns that embraced a sun-darkened face. He glared at the sheriff. "But we came to talk about some of my cattle gone stray, in this direction."

"You calling me a cattle thief?"

"Your sons, at the very least."

"That's worse."

"How is the truth worse?"

"You got a problem with rustling, you should talk with the sheriff. He's right here."

"Might just as soon spit into the wind."

"You hear him talk about you like that, Rufus?" Bentley

looked to the sheriff.

Sheriff Rufus Frazier's gaze stayed fixed on the Vinegar Kid. He kept one hand on his reins and the other on the saddle horn. Wouldn't show any tremor that way, Lucas figured. He knew plenty, enough to err to the side of caution. "I say we tend to this business another day, Sam. You hear me good?"

"I get your drift, if that's what you mean." Bentley could count as good as anyone. He also caught something in the sheriff's tone.

He turned his horse and without bandying another word, gave it his spurs and took off. The others followed at a gallop.

Lucas nearly chuckled to himself, but felt just as glad to be alive. The old bird wasn't daft. No way to come out of a fracas like that unscathed.

They rode hard for a mile or two, until they couldn't see the Bolger place, nor could they see anyone on their heels. Bentley reined up and turned his horse back, sat it and stared off into the distance.

"Now what?" Gabe asked.

"We head to town and wait a spell."

"Don't know why you didn't just lay into them?" Gabe frowned at his father.

Bentley glanced at his son, then the sheriff. "I made it through the war because I learned soon enough that horses can go back as well as forward. I never once took on anyone with more men than I had."

"You gonna hire some more?"

"Not right this moment, Gabe. I got more than one card up my sleeve." He glanced toward the sheriff again, who sat and stared, as patient as winter waiting on spring.

Bentley had said nothing about the rustling, hadn't even looked surprised. Lucas wondered what it would be like to live so long you had to compromise just to survive. He doubted he would last as long out here. Few did. Knowing that made him loosen his gun in its holster, ready for anything.

"What now?" Gabe asked.

The old man squinted into the distance. "We ride to town, then sit . . . and we wait."

CHAPTER TWELVE

Justin peeked out from behind Francis's bulk. He watched the Bentley bunch. Kenedy and his riders talked among themselves, then turned and rode off in the other direction. Probably not a good time for Kenedy to get into anything with the Bentleys, with the sheriff riding among them. Justin took a deep breath, felt he could breathe normally again.

Francis looked behind him and saw Justin standing there in his shadow. He gave him a lopsided grin.

"That was a close one," Justin said.

"I hardly think it's over." Francis turned and headed back for the cabin.

Button had clambered down the ladder, and she came around the house carrying the shotgun.

"Glad you're okay," Justin said.

She looked right at him, and her eyes narrowed. Then she looked away, seemed to want nothing to do with him.

Justin shook his head. "What do you think that was about?"

"You don't know?" Francis looked down at him.

"Nope."

"You showed a yellow stripe."

"Where?"

"Right up your back, where she could see it plain as day."

"How would you know anything about that?"

"Because I have a problem with bravery too. I saw 'shoot to kill' in several of the eyes of those men and thought this might well be my end if something set them all off. My insides were spinning around like dust devils. If it was up to me, I'd have been hiding behind you rather than the other way around."

"Come on. I've seen you do brave things."

"You've seen me do foolish things. That's where I excel. And I do them better and a little quicker with some wine in me, and I'm running out of that."

"Oh." Justin looked up at Francis. Big of a man as he was, Justin could see something now: the shadows of fear just easing from his face. Hard to believe. He glanced around. The others were going back into the house. He saw Button go inside, but she still wouldn't look at him.

The Rangers rode into town, some slapping clouds of the road off their dusters with their hats. The captain had insisted that no man wear what was left of a uniform, whether gray or blue. Many had reverted to homespun or what they could put together or get from stores. Yet they all wore the round silver badges made from Mexican silver pesos, and they all had white hats, or what used to be white before miles of riding and weather of all sorts.

Jobe Jenkins looked around. Not a bad bunch to be riding with. They all would have had at least a notch in their guns if they were prone to do that. None had backed down in a fight yet. Almost all had seen the elephant in a big fight. A few Injun scrapes, dustups with outlaws, and tangles with feud factions and such were just part of the day, and half the fun.

Even ol' Kit would have approved of this bunch. Jobe had only ridden with Kit Carson the once, but it had been a right treat. One of the men had come running to the campfire yelling that the redskins had stolen horses from their remuda. Kit had put down his coffee and left his buffalo steak to yell, "Let's go, boys." No hesitation, and they were all gone and riding hard on the trail.

Kit could be as cautious as it comes when finding his way, had climbed a tree to sit and look around for what seemed hours until he was sure just where they were and should go. But give him horse-stealing Injuns, and he was off in a gallop. Not a second thought.

They'd tracked those Indians too, at last into a box canyon where it could have as easily been a trap for them. But Kit had thought it through while still in the saddle riding, and had figured not. He was right, and they got back their horses and the horses of the Indians as well, the latter having to climb up and out of the canyon, leaving their valued ponies behind. That was Kit, and that was the nature of the bunch Jobe rode with. Captain Marberry wouldn't have any other kind, and he had a nose for picking those wanting to wear the star.

As they rode into town, Jobe had caught the stares from the few people who hurried inside or those who stood to gape. It felt good. They were like a half-lit stick of dynamite rolling into town, and the captain would have it no other way.

Several women moved about on the streets, and they were as different as could be. The wives and such most often turned their heads, looked away. The other women were more prone to blatantly stare. They were out early from whatever house they occupied. Fancy ladies. He thought he could catch the glitter of hard coin in their eyes: silver, or even gold. He doubted the cowhands who came rolling into town with their pay noticed, or cared. But he did. These had the same eyes as gunslingers he'd come across, the kind who would do you in for the price of your spurs. He gave Old Top a nudge with his heels and rode up until he was beside Stubbs, who had turned in his saddle to give a "come here" toss of his head.

"See about fetching us a burro, Jenkins. Ask about switching out a couple of snakebit horses too. Won't hurt." Stubbs pulled in at the general store to get supplies, enough for a long patrol, if needed, while Jobe rode on toward the livery.

He pulled up outside, waited on someone to come outside. The place smelled of horse manure, not all that unpleasant. The building had been put together, it looked, as if from scraps of all manner of boards and bits of lumber from the other buildings that had sprung up to form a town. This place must rank about at the bottom. A man came out into the sun, blinking up at Jobe, who still sat on Old Top.

What sort of man ends up working in a livery? The kind who has perhaps gone out and faced danger and found himself wanting, the kind who could be owned by another, the way this livery was owned by the Bentleys. Sure, it could be honest hard work, but not for this sallow fellow coming toward Jobe, pulling on one long ear lobe.

"Are you Sid?"

"That's what the sign says."

"You have any reason to doubt it?"

"What?"

"I came to see about a burro for a Ranger patrol." Jobe had seen the liveryman staring at his badge. Now his eyes panned up.

"You gonna pay up front?"

"Of course not. You'll get paid by the state. Same as always."

"Well, you fellas kinda like to ride into tough places. I could end up out a burro."

"Then you can bill the state for that."

Sid seemed to think that over. Finally nodded.

"We might need to swap out a couple of horses too. Two of ours are getting over snake bite."

"Should've give 'em whiskey."

"If we'd had any the boys would'a already drunk it."

Sid sighed. He turned to head toward a corral.

Jobe borrowed a rust-colored currycomb off a hook by the livery's wide front door, slipped his hand inside, and started to brush Old Top, who didn't mind at all. Instead, he looked back at him with an encouraging big eye to keep at it.

He lost himself in the task, one he'd done many times, and got to thinking about that boy, the one from the stage. It bothered him some that the boy hadn't been in a lather to go off after the ones who'd kilt his pa. Least that's what he'd of been raring to do.

When he was a boy himself, twelve if he recalled right, he'd been off hunting. He was riding back to the farmstead with a deer haunch hanging off either side of his saddle when he saw the smoke, rushed ahead on a gelding named Mustard, hard to ride as a stallion but tamer now as a gelding. He'd pulled up by the smoking farmhouse, seen what was left of his pa out front, rushed in to find his ma. Both had been scalped. His sister, Tabby, only nine, was a redheaded little sprat so pale she always wore a bonnet out of doors. She was gone, though he looked everywhere. His face wet with tears that shamed him, and ignoring the flames and smoke, he went to the back corner of the cabin and dug with his belt knife until he came to the box. His father had buried it long ago when he took to farming to please Jobe's ma, who had come out from the east to teach school, such as it was. Once he had it out of its hole and shook off the loose dirt, he opened the box. Inside he saw the rolled leather of his pa's gun belt, wrapped around his old Navy pistol. A heavy gun for a boy, but he'd strapped it on. He took along everything he'd need to keep it loaded and staggered out from the smoke.

The cabin collapsed as he mounted Mustard, and he left his own pa out for the buzzards. His insides heated up like a campfire, he rode out, circled the house, picked up the trail, and started off as fast as he could go and still keep sight of the trail.

So choked up he could hardly see straight, he slowed after the first few hasty miles and made himself think. What was bothering him? What niggled?

Well, for one thing, he realized the trail he followed was of shod horses. Unless the horses were stolen, that was odd. The arrows he seen back at the farm, now that he thought hard on it, had been a mix of Cherokee and Comanche. Not likely either.

It was a head-scratcher, sure enough. It made him slow down, be more careful, even though they surely had Tabby. Then he lost their trail and had to cast about for the better part of an hour.

He struck the trail again where it crossed the San Marcos at the mouth of Mule Creek and followed it northwestward up toward the head of York's Creek. From there it wove through the mountains to the Guadalupe, and up the stream he knew only as Johnson's Fork, a principal mountain tributary to the Guadalupe on the north side, that led down a junction with the Llano. The trail peeled off from there and led up the back slope all the way to a mesa. He knew the men who'd killed his family were camped there, could see the smoke of their fire.

Rather than ride up the slope side where they could see him, he tied Mustard to a mesquite limb and started up the cliff side, watching for snakes, since there were several crevasses and holes under rocks that looked snaky as all get-out.

Nothing he'd done in his life was harder than the scramble up the wrong side of that mesa. Every sticker seemed to latch onto him, every rock give his knees or elbows a knock or a clip. When he at last got to the rim and pulled himself up and over, the sun was easing down over the horizon in a majestic spray of oranges, pinks, and fading blue. He could make out one of the men on top of Tabby, raping her. White men, just as he'd thought. The other two were turned that way. Jobe knew to take them first. He eased closer, shot one in the back of the head. The other was drawing as he turned. Jobe shot him in the chest. The one over Tabby was half scrambling to his feet, and at the same time crawling toward a rifle that lay on the ground near him, but not near enough. Jobe's first shot caught him in the crotch. Maybe not an accident, at that. The next shot went in one ear and sprayed parts of him across Tabby.

Jobe never knew whether Tabby did what she did because she didn't recognize Jobe, or because she did. She got to her feet and still only half dressed ran across to the cliff's edge and dove.

He'd scalped those men, all three of them. Had thrown up twice while doing it. He should have gone through their pockets and taken their guns, but couldn't bring himself to touch a thing. He had taken a couple of brands from their fire, used them to guide himself down the slope side. Tabby had fallen not far from where he'd tied Mustard. Jobe collapsed beside her body. In the morning he'd buried her as best he could. Rocks piled high over her to keep the coyotes away. Then he'd ridden off, feeling as hollow inside as he'd ever felt.

Still, he couldn't figure why that boy hadn't wanted to go after those men who'd kilt his pa. He sought to shake it off, but it still bothered him some.

Sid came back, leading two horses and a burro. "How will these do?"

Jobe lifted the hooves of each and examined each shoe. "You can take back the half lame one. We already have one of those. It's why we need fresh steeds."

Sid grumped, but he knew which one to peel away and take back to the corral.

When he came back the next time he had a horse worth riding, a sorrel that looked ready and able to take to the trail.

"Have you shoed any horses lately?" Jobe kept an eye on Sid as he asked.

"Nope. Why d'you ask?"

The man was lying. Wasn't any reason to lie, but he was. Jobe had made a study of faces and if Sid dragging a foot and looking down as soon as he'd answered wasn't a tell, he didn't know what. Lying. But why?

Sid waved Jobe inside to a corner of the building where a mere slope of board served as a desk.

Sid held out a scrap of paper. Jobe took it, looked it over then dipped pen in ink and signed the paper, a skill he had, thanks to a school-teaching Ma. If Sid tried to dummy a different bill later when he submitted it, the captain could straighten that out, and he would.

"The old captain, Bentley, he owns this place, don't he, this livery?"

"Yeah. No secret there. Why're you askin' about him?"

"Just wondered. I heard a rumor that old man Bentley was tight as the bark on a willow tree, had his original first halfpenny."

"That's true enough. So?"

"Seems like he'd be making a bigger fuss out of the stage being robbed since most the money was his."

"Oh, he's been carrying on plenty. He's been all over Sheriff Frazier 'bout that. Man rode out there. Wasn't much to see or make of it."

"I doubt there was. Not even the tracks leading from there right back to this town."

Sid gave a visible jerk. Jobe couldn't have jabbed at Sid with a hot branding iron and got more of a jolt. The man had twitched half out of his skin. Jobe would truly like to get this man into a poker game. He was playing hunches, and Sid was rising like a trout to bait.

Jobe led the burrow and the two fresh steeds up the street. A group of men came riding in and tied up outside the saloon. Jobe was pretty sure the stout red-faced fellow in a rebel-gray officer's hat was the old man himself. Not a single one of those with him looked the least bit happy, and that included Lucas Brent who the Rangers had given a lift not long back.

One rider peeled off and rode over to the sheriff's office. He tied up there and went inside.

Jobe tied up Old Top and the burro and horses at the general store, beside the horses of Stubbs and the others. Then he eased across the street toward the saloon. Once he stood by the row of horses, he leaned and took a peek inside the door. The whole bunch was clustered at the bar with glasses of beer. Looked like the old man wasn't going to spring for anything stronger. Must have plans.

He eased back and went along the row of horses. He knew enough to approach each with the right care, spending a moment introducing himself to the horse before he slid back to lift a left hind hoof. Fourth horse in a row, a sorrel, he found what he was looking for, a new nail in the shoe, and a mark where one had been bent over.

He let the hoof down and went across the street, ducked inside the general store. It took a second or two for his eyes to adjust. Then he saw Stubbs at the counter, ticking off the things he'd asked for. Jobe waved a hand for him to come over.

"You get a burro?"

"Yep."

"Start loading, boys." He leaned closer to Jobe. "What's in your craw, Jenkins?"

"Has old man Bentley been making any kind of fuss over that stagecoach being robbed?"

"Not as much as the stage company. They've put up a reward. Seems Captain Bentley filed a claim. I just sent a wire to

Captain Marberry, and he wired me right back. Why?"

"Do you think there's a chance he might have held up the stage himself, then made the claim?"

"Doesn't seem likely. Man was straight as an arrow. Tight as a mouthful of lemon, but bone honest. What have you got?"

Jobe told him about the tracks leading to town and the horse in the Bentley string that matched the hoofprints.

"Well, I'll be flayed." Stubbs lifted his hat to scratch at his head. "Might could be the boys are feeling Papa's pinch and did it on their own. But, mind you, we have nothing in the way of any kind of proof."

"What should we do?"

"Well, it's a pickle, and we can't expect anything from the sheriff. He's tucked up drinking from the Bentley trough. From what I've learned so far this town is divided and confused. Most are used to the Bentleys being the so-called royalty. But some are jaded by the Bentley ways and are adjusting to Kenedy being the new money, even though he's from Massachusetts. Don't think money don't talk, no matter where it comes from."

"All we got's a suspicion. Right?"

"Well, you keep an eye on those horses. Let me know who mounts the sorrel. Okay?"

Jobe leaned in the shadow against the side of the general store when the Bentley bunch emerged from the saloon and mounted. He leaned out enough to notice Esau climb up on the sorrel. Interesting. Jobe would have liked to follow them. He watched them round up the sheriff once again and wondered where they were headed. He would have liked to follow them a spell. But he had his orders.

As soon as they were out of sight, and before their dust had even settled, he mounted Old Top and headed off to catch up with Stubbs and the others. They left a big enough trail. Not hard to follow.

He'd only ridden a half dozen miles when he reined in Old Top, looked down at the trail and couldn't believe his eyes. On top of the prints the Rangers had left, the prints of unshod horses began to appear on top of the Ranger sign.

Jobe backtracked until they came onto the trail the Rangers were leaving, followed that off a mile until he came to a roughly butchered calf, one that wore a badly changed Bentley brand on top of the Kenedy brand. So they had meat. What the hell were they up to?'

He rode back until he picked up the Ranger trail again. Sure enough, the Indian sign was still there, on top of the shod horse prints. It could mean only one thing. Bent Feather had come around behind the Rangers and was on their tail now, safely behind them. Maybe he had been leading Stubbs and the others in circles. But now he was quietly pursuing them.

The hunters had become the hunted. Jobe had been on trails most of his life and only twice, once with a wounded mountain lion, and another time with a bear, had the tables been turned on him. This was the third time, and Stubbs wasn't going to like it a bit, if it wasn't too late. Jobe gave Old Top his heels. It would be up to him to get there first.

Chapter Thirteen

Sara looked up from where she was cutting vegetables for a stew and saw Justin sitting glum at one of the wooden chairs at the table watching her. She rested one hand for a moment on the wooden surface. The table's top had a texture from being much used and lived on, a chopping and cutting block as well as where they ate. She had to do all her kitchen work at the table, then scrub it down with the fresh water Justin had fetched from the well.

Scamp squatted over in one corner, closer to the fireplace than Sara might have preferred. Scamp was cleaning and loading all the weapons, a chore he seemed to do well as a result of much practice. He swabbed out the muzzleloader and tamped in a new round. The two of them switched back and forth between the shotgun and the muzzleloader. It was a wonder a big gun like that didn't knock little Button flat, but she seemed to be of hardy enough stock to take it well. Sara figured that Justin probably wondered for a moment where Button might be. Missy sat across the table from Justin and washed the vegetables and handed them to her mother.

Everyone had learned to pitch in, and Justin might be itching to share any of the family's burden. He still seemed a guest in their eyes, though, not part of them all the way yet. Living like this could seem to be dreary, Sara knew well enough, but he hadn't found it so. Perhaps their having to race to a window with a gun from time to time took some of the dull away.

Justin stood.

"Where are you going?" Sara asked.

"Out. Maybe Button needs a hand."

Sara grinned to herself. Button had sure enough been in a huff. If there was anything that would make some boys sit up and take notice, it was when the light of unfettered adoration went out of a girl's eyes, however temporarily.

Scamp looked up as Justin went out the door. He'd been more than a little disappointed in Justin too.

Sara went back to peeling and cutting vegetables. Give him time. He just got out this way. The boy will find his metal. Or not. Being out here tested a person in ways he hadn't run into yet. Well, he had now.

Justin picked his way through the dirt behind the house. He looked for her in the vegetable fields, finally spotted her over by the goat shed where he'd spent the night. Button had changed back to her rough everyday wear and had a sack of feed over her shoulder, which she dropped just inside the shed. She picked up a pitchfork that rested against the shed's side and started to throw the grass and other gathered fodder over to the goats. All this land around them was Aunt Sara's, but the growth was not enough to graze upon unless they built fences on the extremes of her land. The chances were the cattlemen on either side would tear those down so their cattle could get at what little there was.

Cactus and bunchgrass scattered among the loose rock and sandy soil. It was a hard place to live upon, and sooner or later the people who lived on it got as hard. Though it hadn't caught up with Aunt Sara yet, and it certainly hadn't Button, whose smooth skin held only a light patina of brown from the sun. She looked up, saw Justin coming, turned her back to him, and kept working.

He hung back, no longer even slightly sure of himself. He had acted badly. He knew that. And people out here were quick to judge. But he had this coming. Justin realized that when it came to taking action, doing the right thing no matter what, he was no better than his father. That was as low as anyone could go, and he slithered along on this path like a snake on its belly. At least he felt as low and worthless.

Lost in his thoughts, he barely heard Button's startled half scream. He looked up. A man had walked around the back of the shed and towered over Button, a rough cowhand of a man, and he had his arms around her, holding her hands down at her sides. She was trying to kick at him, but he twisted so her lashing heels caught only air.

Justin heard men laughing. His head turned to the right, and he saw a row of men on horses on the other side of the goat corral. They were the same men who'd ridden up to the house earlier. They'd come back, and he could see the sheriff with them. But the sheriff just sat on his horse, looking half sad and half bored. He did nothing.

"What are you doing? What do you want?" Button struggled in the man's hands.

"You gonna need a hand there, Esau?" one of the men on horseback called over to the man.

"No. I got her. But she's one little bobcat and a half."

In spite of tugging and wrestling to get free with all she had, Button's eyes locked with Justin's for a brief moment. In them he saw anger, and worse, disdain, not at the man who held her, but at Justin. She couldn't have kicked him or flung manure at him and stung him worse.

Without even knowing what he was doing he ran forward, yelling and swinging his fists.

Esau's eyes widened as Justin slammed into him at full tilt, whaling away with his small fists. To Justin, it felt as though he were hitting the wind and sun-hardened, boarded sides of the shed. The bigger man just laughed, but at least he let go of Button. He drew his gun and brought it down hard on Justin's forehead in what seemed a sudden red blur of pain. The next thing he knew, Justin was on the ground, dirty, with a trickle of blood running down over one eye. He saw Esau grab for Button.

Justin scrambled to his feet and threw himself at Esau again. He barely got in a couple of useless swings when the barrel of the gun came down on him. This time, when Justin shook his head and tried to rise, he seemed to see two of Button before she wavered and came together. He shook his head, put his hands on the ground, and started to push himself up again.

"Stay down!" Button screamed. "Just stay down. He'll kill you, Justin."

"That's okay," Justin muttered. He'd never been drunk, but this is what it must feel like. He staggered, and his legs seemed uncertain as he tried to force himself back toward Esau.

"Leave the boy alone." This was a big, deep voice, and it boomed from just inside the shed. Francis came rushing out from where he must have been sneaking a nap.

Esau spun, one hand grasping Button's upper arm, the other swinging his pistol up toward Francis. But a fist the size of a small ham was already swinging toward Esau and caught him just in front of his left ear. Esau dropped to the ground like a rain-soaked blanket. His pistol fell to his side.

Button bent and came back up with the gun, but before she could raise it, Justin heard the clicks of half a dozen hammers being pulled back. The barrels pointed at Francis.

"What the blue-eyed devil is going on out here?" Sara held her Winchester and was stomping across the yard toward them from the house. Justin saw the barrel of the muzzle loader poke out a window of the old fort and point at the men.

"We've got papers of indenture," Captain Bentley shouted. "Perfectly legal. When you can't pay what you owe, we have a right to collect as best we can."

"Why are you doing this?" Sara shouted back. But she had to know. Bentley had squeezed out almost every other homesteader in the area. She was the last of them.

Justin rubbed the blood out of his eye and stood on shaky legs. He expected at any second to hear a volley of shots gunning them all down.

"We're taking the girl." Bentley was looking down at the ground, though, where Esau had yet to stir.

"I know what you want with her. You'll have to kill us all first, like the low-life vermin you are." She kicked Esau where he lay, and he didn't twitch.

Justin started to wonder if Francis had killed him with that punch. It was possible. He'd seen mule kicks that weren't as hard as that punch had been.

Sara raised her rifle, and Button lifted the pistol she held. Bentley saw that and the rifle pointing their way from the house. "You're outnumbered, Sara. We have the law on our side here."

"Such as it is around here." She spoke between clenched teeth.

Justin blinked and rubbed at the blood that flowed. He felt light-headed, but expected to be shot where he stood at any second. The tension was as thick and taut as he'd ever felt.

"There might be another way," Lucas said.

Heads turned to look at Lucas. He and the sheriff were the only ones not to have drawn their guns.

"Well?" Bentley snapped.

"Maybe the boy has something of value, something worth having instead of the girl," Lucas said.

Justin knew in an instant what he meant. He must have seen more than he'd let on.

"What the hell're you talking about?"

"A map." Lucas nodded toward Justin. "He has a treasure map, a real one. Don't you, boy?"

Justin glanced toward Francis, then Sara, and finally Button. They were all staring at him.

"You're not joshing me now, are you?" Bentley's voice had settled into a low growl. He still stared at the fallen Esau.

"Nope. Justin there may have something worth your while. After all, you can't squeeze blood from a turnip."

"What's to keep us from just taking it? The way we took the girl." Bentley glanced toward Lucas.

"Because we are men of honor."

One of the men started to laugh.

"Stow that, Gabe. Not the time or place." Captain Bentley sounded like someone who'd forgotten how to laugh himself, if he'd ever known. He had a voice like gravel being kicked up by steel-shod hooves.

"First, check my boy."

Button bent closer to where Esau lay. "He's breathing." She didn't touch him, and she let a curl of disgust show at the corner of her mouth.

Justin could see the man's chest rise and fall. One side of his face was already pink and starting to become tinged with purple. Seemed fair enough, considering the way Justin's own head felt.

Bentley let out a huff of air. He turned to Lucas. "What makes you think this boy's piece of paper's worth anything? We get men pouring through here every day with maps or rumors of one kind or another way to get rich. Most of these men are dumb as fence posts and their maps aren't worth the paper they're on. What makes this scrap different?"

"Perhaps Francis there could tell you. He knows a thing or two about maps."

Francis looked around at the others, Sara and her kids, as

well as at Justin. Part of him seemed reluctant to let the map from within his grasp, but the other part realized it was as good as their lives here. It was all they had to trade that was worth a hill of beans.

"When the Union troops pulled out of some of these hayseed forts that dotted the frontier to hold the Indians back, they moved quick, figured they'd go home, whip the southern states into line, and be right back out here. They took what they could and buried what was too heavy to carry quickly. Given a choice, they hauled ammo but left behind some of the payroll gold."

"And?" Bentley said.

"The boy's uncle was the quartermaster, only one who knew where. He's the one who made the map. There's every reason to believe this one's authentic."

Bentley sat and looked away for a moment, and finally came to a conclusion. He turned to glare at Sara. "It looks like we have a talking point. Are you willing to talk?"

She looked at Justin. "It's not mine to give."

Justin didn't hesitate. He stepped forward. "Look, if I give it to you, will you swear to leave Aunt Sara and everyone here alone?"

"I don't need to swear to nothing."

"You will if you want to see that map. I've hidden it, and you won't get a glimpse of it unless you agree." He had tried very hard to make his voice firm and unflinching, but even he heard a waver to his words. "Swear it to your sheriff there."

"Okay, kid, but this map had better deliver." Bentley looked to Sheriff Frazier. "You're the witness here, Rufus."

The sheriff just nodded. He had stared in stony silence the while, and there didn't seem to be anything he wanted to say now.

Justin turned, and his first steps nearly betrayed him and sent him tumbling. He felt woozy and sick to his stomach. He slipped inside the shadows of the shed, and Francis followed him. He watched Justin go through the motions of going to a hiding place. Then Justin lifted a pant leg and took the folded map out from inside his boot top.

"Look, kid. You don't have to do this. The map was your all, everything your father left to you."

"Yes, I do have to do this," Justin said. "For a number of reasons, all of them the right ones." He turned and started back out from the shed, holding up the map.

CHAPTER FOURTEEN

Jobe bent closer to the trail, took in each bent blade of grass and hoofprint. As the prints became more distinct, less softened by the steady blow of wind, he slowed. Before he crossed the next low rise ahead, he led Old Top over to a stand of chaparral, full of agarita and everything else with any kind of thorn, and tied the reins. He slid his carbine out of its scabbard and crouched low to ease up to the crest and peek over. Good thing he did.

Below he could see the other Rangers starting to set up camp. Between him and them he saw the Indians spread out, two already slipping in a crawl over toward the remuda where they could get at the horses and burro. He had to hand it to that Bent Feather for daring, trying to steal horses from a group like these Rangers, but so far the edge was all on the side of the Comanche and Kiowa warriors.

He had little time. The lead Comanche nearest the horses was flat on the ground and squeezing through a pair of yuccas. All the other warriors were poised to start shooting.

Jobe carefully sighted and drew a bead on the moving warrior, leading him just a bit. He slowly squeezed the trigger, felt the rifle buck in his hands, watched every Indian head snap his way. The Rangers dove for cover, and in an instant turned from a helpless bunch about to be slaughtered into a fighting unit that outnumbered the ambushing warriors.

A shot from a rifle threw dirt up from the ground in front of

Jobe. As many shots were aimed at the Rangers below, but none of them came from where they were before. The Rangers in turn fired up at the Indians. Jobe ducked low so he wouldn't be hit by a stray shot from either side.

He shifted his position, moving over behind a red-and-brown boulder. Subtle as he'd been, someone was watching, and a bullet ricocheted off the rock and sent a spray of sandstone flying into the air and down over him. Jobe ducked lower.

Below a flurry of shots, far more from the Ranger side than the Indian, filled the afternoon air. He could smell gunpowder, hear the rustling as the Comanche warriors scurried to change positions, and in a few moments more he heard the pounding of unshod horses headed away from them, far to his left. They had cut and run right now when the winds of advantage had shifted. He gave a begrudging tip of his hat to Bent Feather. But he looked with care before he dared rise and show himself to the Rangers far below, several of who were already saddling up, getting ready for the chase.

The body of one of the Comanche lay where Jobe had shot him. The others had all gotten away. A couple of the Rangers were wrapping quick bandages from torn shirttails around a place here and there where they'd been winged. But they were all present and able.

As Jobe rode down to join in with the others, Stubbs was shouting, "Grace and Simmons, stay with the camp and the burro. Like as not an Injun like Bent Feather might just loop back on us and have a go at our supplies while we were chasing him." It was a high mark of respect for an Indian for Stubbs to give, but Jobe had to agree.

Bo and Zed didn't look happy to miss out on the chase. But, truth of it was, Bo was best at tracking and shooting from a stance, not from horseback and riding hard. Zed would just have to wait for another time, too.

Stubbs gave a wave and the rest of the Rangers took off as fast as they could go. Jobe rode hard and not only kept up, but eased toward the front of the group. Old Top could be competitive, and now wasn't a bad time for that. But doubt stewed in Jobe's mind about whether they could catch Bent Feather. He was turning out to be just about the wiliest redskin Jobe had ever come across.

Sure enough, they lost the trail twice when the Indians had seemed to go up a stream then down it, and a while later they had pulled the same trick the other way around. Finally the Rangers lost the trail altogether when the tracks led them up to a stretch of hard flat rock and disappeared. No matter which way they cast about, they couldn't find the hint of a sign of where they had gone. Maybe they should have brought Bo after all.

"Well, that does it, boys. Let's get back to camp before that rascal shows up there. I'll want a double watch tonight, and I don't mean for you to sit there and stare at the moon, but take a walking patrol now and again, and keep an eye on them damn horses."

Stubbs waved an arm, and they all headed back to the camp, not as fast this time, but keeping a wary eye about all the way.

Jobe rode up beside Stubbs, but didn't try to trade words with him. Stubbs looked a little outfoxed and snakebit at the moment, and seemed to want to mull over what had just happened for a stretch of the ride back.

CHAPTER FIFTEEN

Gabe and Lucas, of Bentley's bunch, came across through the goat corral and picked up Esau to carry him like a limp rag back to the others. They paused and Gabe held out a hand to Justin for the map, but he handed it to Lucas instead, even though Lucas was the one who had given its existence away. Justin tried to feel bad about losing the map and all of the opportunity it held, but his eyes swept the others: Sara and Button, even Francis. Not much to see there. Sad, but alive. Certainly not gleeful. But for a second he felt good, that he might just this once have done the right thing. Then his eyes closed, everything went black, and he could feel himself falling.

Justin's eyes fluttered open and he saw Aunt Sara dabbing a cloth in a bucket and then rubbing at his face with the damp cloth that came away pink when she lifted it. Scamp hovered close at Sara's elbow. He looked half worried and half proud. The room seemed dim, just the dancing flicker of the light from the fireplace lighting it. "How long . . . ?"

"Most of the afternoon," Sara said. "We were pretty concerned there for a spell. You got konked on the noggin right good there a couple of times. We're glad you did what you could to buy us some time, but you shouldn't have."

"Yes," he managed to say, "I should."

Across the room, sitting in the shadows, he could make out Button. He didn't know what to make of her expression.

Uncertain, he guessed. Well, heck, he felt a little the same himself.

Missy tugged at her mother's elbow, perhaps a touch jealous at the attention someone else was getting.

Justin could feel his head throb to the beat of his heart. His head felt twice its size, his heart still small and a little bitter. He seemed to see things more clearly than usual and doubted for the first time that he would ever amount to much.

A large head poked in from the other side of Sara. Francis. He held a tin coffee mug, and Justin could guess what it held. "You feeling any better, little fella?" he slurred. "Sorry about the map and all. Damned shame to lose that."

"Language, Mister Francis. Language, please."

Francis muttered as he moved a step back from Sara's glare. "But it saved our bacon. Tell you that."

"Scamp, would you kindly show Mister Francis out to his quarters please?" Sara looked back down, kept daubing at Justin's head, which felt like one large dried scab.

Despite his throbbing head, Justin thought part of his aunt Sara looked as delicate and fine as a bone-china teacup, while the other side could be as flinty as stone ever gets.

"Have I mentioned what a fine and handsome woman you are when riled, Sara?" Francis's voice came from farther back, out of Justin's sight.

"Scamp. Get him out of here."

"But the boys have hidden the blankets."

"I 'spect you'll stay plenty warm enough."

Francis moved back closer, to wave at Justin with one hand. He raised his other hand, which held the wine. An inch or so still sloshed around in the bottom of the bottle. He nodded. Then his giant head lifted and faded out of Justin's sight.

"Your friend is something." Sara rubbed harder. Justin flinched and she eased up.

"He's not really a friend."

"I thought as much. But he did lay out that Esau right proper." She hesitated. "Ah, men. My Luther wasn't any tougher than a child-strength fever. While your uncle Roger could work like any number of hives of bees, and was as good a craftsman as you could find, he had his share of oddities and quirks. I just hope you can stay with the glimmer of promise you've showed."

Justin tried to parse out what she could possibly mean by that, but his heavy eyes closed, and that was all he knew. He dreamed, but it was all bent rainbows and horses that walked sideways. His head throbbed all the while like so many Indian war drums beating in the distance.

He woke to the sound of Scamp easing out of his blanket. Justin had insisted he was fit enough to go sleep in the goat shed, and the women had been a bit relieved by that. He'd wobbled some as Scamp had helped him out to the shed. It was a cooler night, so they pulled the blankets from Francis, who was hogging them again, and pushed him to one side. He mumbled in his sleep, but didn't wake.

Once up and moving about, Justin caught up with Scamp in time to help draw water and carry it to the house. Then they gave the goats some feed and were out in the vegetable patch, weeding by hand when Sara stuck her head out the door and found them. There were pumpkins, gourds, rows of onions, and all manner of root vegetables. Weeds, as they always did, seemed to find a way to crowd in and try to encroach. Scamp used the hoe, and Justin made do with a shovel he jabbed at the weeds and twisted their roots loose from their holds.

A low mist seemed to rise from the ground as the sun heated and baked off the dew. Birds chattered in the distance and the goats made contented sounds as they tucked into their morning meal.

Francis came plodding toward the house, rubbing his arms with his hands. "Don't know why I wake each morning with the chilblains. That shed gets colder than a mother-in-law's heart."

"Careful of your language, Mister Francis."

"Why, look at that boy working away," he said, glancing toward where Justin worked up a morning sweat in the garden. "Perhaps he's taking to farm life out here, after all."

"He does seem to have had a change of heart." Sara brushed the hair out of her eyes with one hand.

"Maybe he could have used a rap on the head before."

"I doubt that's what's done it, but if it was, I'd try a rap of the shovel over your head."

"What makes you say a thing like that?" Francis shook his tousled head. "And is there coffee yet?"

"I guess you know we're back where we were. There's no way we can pay the taxes if Bentley and the others keep freezing us out. Whatever was in that map was our only hope, thin as that was."

"Probably it will all make more sense after a good breakfast," Francis hinted.

"I doubt that. But come inside. You're still company, such as that is."

CHAPTER SIXTEEN

Jobe stirred in his bedroll, then tossed off the blanket. It was light enough to see some of the others up and moving about. He could darn sure smell the coffee. Probably young Zed doing that chore. The way they did it was to put a pint cupful of ground coffee beans into the pot and let that boil for half an hour. Some claimed it could eat its way through an anvil, or at least bedrock. The saying in Texas was that the only way to tell if coffee was strong enough was to put an iron wedge in the coffeepot. If it floated, the coffee was strong enough. But a big cup of it at that strength with no milk would keep anyone alert for a considerable spell.

It felt good to be in camp and back to a routine breakfast: bread cooked in a skillet and a big slab of beefsteak fried. That calf had been just lying there and they'd butchered off enough for as long as it would keep, a day or two. Then they'd go back to using the slabs of bacon still in the bags the burro carried. Might as well chase those redskins with the same beef they'd killed. There was some justice in that, and it was mighty tasty too, the way Jobe figured. And it sat real comfy in your stomach for a long day in the saddle.

Zed and the others went upstream of the rill beside the camp to rinse off their plates and cups, then they mounted. Jobe felt ready to ride all day if need be.

"How long you think 'fore we join back up with the rest of

the Frontier Battalion?" Zed asked Jobe as they rode along at a trot.

"Don't know. I expect once we've cleared up this small Injun bunch or caught us a stage robber. Either way. Stubbs wants some kind of feather in his cap."

They crossed over into the Kenedy spread and had only gone a mile or two when Bo waved an arm for Jobe to ride up on point and have a look.

"Look at these prints. They go one way one minute and another the next. Then they disappear, reappear later, only not where you'd expect."

"Hmmm." Jobe bent closer.

"What do you make of tracks like that?" Bo lifted his hat to sweep his hair back and put the hat back on.

This stretch of tracks seemed to go both ways at once, then they'd trail off, loop back, and start off in another direction. If Jobe hadn't known better, he'd suspect those Injuns had gotten hold of some firewater somewhere.

"I don't know what to make of them."

"Blamedest trail I ever struck." Bo bent closer. "Do you think it's possible these dang redskins are playing some kind of game?"

"I don't know. Could be Bent Feather's lost."

"That Injun is a lot of things, but being lost isn't one of them."

Jobe sat his horse and looked ahead. No telling what Bent Feather was up to, but whatever it was, it was on purpose. He wished he could figure out what that purpose was. Indians like him might go to reservation for the better part of a year, then ride out on the renegade path, just to disrupt and pillage what they could. He shook his head. It had been a busy few days. They had run into everything but Mexican desperadoes, and he wouldn't be surprised if they crossed paths with those next.

Bo rode on up ahead, waved an arm when he'd picked up

what he thought was the proper trail again.

Jobe signaled back to Stubbs, and the rest of the Rangers rode on again.

As soon as the Rangers had almost passed on out of sight, a head lifted from behind a stand of prickly pear cactus on a low ridge just above where they had been. Sleeping Bear watched the Rangers until the last one was out of sight. He eased upright and then went back to where his paint horse stood waiting. He hopped on the horse and rode across the open range in a line that kept him out of sight of the Rangers, but heading straight for where Bent Feather and the others waited. The wind lifted his twin braids of hair and tugged at his leggings as his horse picked its way up a slope at full gallop. Bent Feather had chosen him since he was the youngest, lightest, and fastest rider of them. Also, Bent Feather didn't fully depend on the two Kiowa warriors who were part of all that was left of his dwindling war party.

As Sleeping Bear skirted a long abandoned buffalo wallow and hit a seam at the edge of buffalo grass and the gravel that led down to a small stream, a roadrunner came strutting out of its cover and ran along beside him before peeling off and going its own way. That was the name he wanted for his warrior name. Roadrunner. He took that as a sign, a very good sign. Not for him the way his father died, broken and with no more fight, buried on the reservation. He was ready for a warrior name now, to die a warrior if he had to.

He didn't slow until he got to the slope that led up to the hill that overlooked the Kenedy ranch house. Sleeping Bear hopped off and led his horse over to tie it beside the others. He eased up to the top of the slope, lowered himself as he came to the crest, and nodded when Bent Feather looked his way.

Below, the men were saddling up. All of them. Every able

man on the Kenedy spread, most of them gunslingers as well as cowhands. Once mounted, they headed off toward where Kenedy's land turned into that of the Bentley spread.

Sleeping Bear could see no movement below. Only a mere servant or two had stayed behind and were left at the ranch house.

The Comanche waited until the men were out of sight and beyond hearing the sound of a gunshot. Then Bent Feather signaled for his men to get their horses and attack.

CHAPTER SEVENTEEN

Gabe held the map while he and Esau rode up on point. They best knew the landmarks. Lucas and the other hired men weren't from here, so Lucas watched the two sons confer from time to time, then ride ahead again at a gallop. Lucas glanced back during one of the pauses, and saw Bentley chafing as his sons followed the treasure map's landmarks.

Lucas nearly let out a disgusted puff of breath. Treasure map. The only thing that gave the yarn any glue was the fact that the boy's uncle had been a Union quartermaster. It was entirely possible that those bluecoats had buried a bulky payroll, expecting to come back soon and reclaim it. He'd heard of worse judgment. Still, a treasure map. Even the idea sounded funny. Yet the old man's eyes glittered rapaciously with greed. Already rich and a miser when it came to his own sons. He was sure something.

"You'd better hope this pans out for you," Lucas said as he rode up closer to Captain Bentley. "If it doesn't, I ride out of here."

"None of the others have been so insistent about getting paid up front."

"None of them are as good as me."

"We'll know if that holds water when you get a chance to prove your worth." Bentley spurred his stallion and rode up to be closer to his boys, perhaps to chime in about the clues and landmarks.

★ ★ ★ ★ ★

Jobe saw the birds first, their wings a V; not hawks or eagles. Buzzards. Then he saw a few wisps of smoke lifting upward, only to be jerked away by the breeze that swayed the tops of the live oaks.

Bo, ahead, reined in and waved for Jobe, who gave his heels to Old Top and rode up at a clip. Stubbs glanced their way and kicked his horse into a gallop as well.

As soon as Jobe drew up to Bo, he could see smoke coming from what must have been the quarters for the ranch hands. The fire was dying down already and just a few blackened sticks were all that remained of the building. A fire had started on the house as well, but it was mostly made of two-foot-thick baked bricks, and just a few tendrils and wisps of flame and smoke flickered in the wind around it. First time he'd ever laid eyes on the Kenedy ranch house, and it wasn't showing at its best.

A body lay out in the yard between the house and the stables. Looked like a woman from here. Leastways Jobe thought he could make out part of an apron.

"Let Bo and me go down first, have a slow, careful look before everyone rides through. Okay, Sarge?"

Stubbs nodded, his face grim. "What are you thinking?"

"Nothing yet. The most amazing bunch of nothing I've ever thought. I hope to know more soon."

He and Bo rode down a ways, then dismounted and tied their horses at a rail beside a trough that ran beside the well, a place horses could be watered. They went across on foot, carefully, looking around. Bo took his hat off, ran his fingers through his hair to pull it back. As Jobe moved closer, he could hear the rasp as Bo swept his hard hand over the stubble on his chin.

"What the hell?" Jobe said.

"You got that right. Wind wouldn't have wiped out every

trace. But there isn't a single print of any kind around this woman."

"Servant, you figure? Cook, maybe?"

"Probably. Let's look around." Bo bent closer to the ground, headed toward the stable. Jobe was right behind when they came to a young Mexican hand, his skull crushed in with a branding iron. No prints around him either.

"This ain't right," Bo said.

"That iron is more not right. It's a Bentley branding iron."

Bo leaned close. "Damn. You're right."

"Let's not touch anything."

"Not that it matters. Not much to touch." Bo stood up straight. He started walking toward the ranch house.

Stubbs and the others came riding down to them. They'd waited long enough. "What'd you boys find?"

"You wanna tell him?" Bo said.

"He'll figure it out."

"There's nothing here, except the tracks you two made." Stubbs glanced around. "The rest of you, spread out. Look around. Let me know what you find."

He moved closer to Bo and Jobe. "Any ideas?"

"I'm as stumped as I've ever been," Bo admitted.

"You don't think the wind swept everything clean?"

"Nope."

"You, Jenkins?"

Jobe stared off at the sky. Aside from the buzzards still circling, a few just now settling into the bare branches of nearby trees, he could see a separate group of buzzards circling a ways off. "Give me a moment of two, if you will. Poke around all you want. I doubt you'll find much."

He took off and rode out into the heart of the Kenedy spread, a fair bit of rock, sand, and cactus. Not near as much grass as back in the buffalo days, when the Indians burned off the fields each year to ensure there would be plenty of grass the next year to lure the buffalo back down south. Now there was little or nothing to lure. Wild scrub and chaparral sprang up pretty much at will.

He'd give Kenedy this. There wasn't a fence in any direction yet. Jobe skirted a wide chaparral of agarita, mesquite, and cactus that ran in a tangle down into an arroyo and up the other sloping side. Hell of a time getting a calf out of that.

Old Top crested the next rise and Jobe could see it now. One or two of the buzzards had landed, were taking a tentative step or two toward where the dead calf lay. Flies had found it. They buzzed around the open side where the ribs had been cut out. Someone had bothered to take the liver, and the tongue. Again, there wasn't a single track in the area. Jobe looked down from where he sat his horse. He shook his head. Only one thing it could be. That damned Bent Feather. But to what end?

He turned and rode back toward the ranch house. Before he even got there, he saw a large cloud of dust. It was approaching the ranch house too, coming from the other direction. As he got closer he could make out the herd of cattle, and drovers driving it. Some rode at the back end, covered in dust, but making sure none strayed. He figured the fellow up at the front to be Kenedy. And if Jobe were asked to bet, without even taking a closer look, he'd bet all of the cattle would bear the Bentley brand rigged over what once had been the Kenedy mark. Or most of them. The old man had probably taken a few more just to even things out. This whole area was about to burst into one of those cattle wars that had ripped counties apart before.

Jobe's first instinct was to ride over to Kenedy and give him some kind of warning about what to expect at his ranch house. Then he thought better of that. Stubbs would want to handle that. Besides, like as not, Kenedy was half in the middle of something that looked pretty close to rustling, even if most the cattle were his own.

As the herd neared the ranch, Kenedy seemed to sense something was amiss, perhaps saw the birds or smoke. His horse broke into a gallop as he gave it his spurs. Two more figures pulled apart from the hands managing the herd.

Jobe got back to the ranch at the same time Kenedy did. Stubbs had tied his horse and stood looking down at the woman.

He looked up to Kenedy as he reined in.

"Two more dead. Boy at the stable. Some old man out back of the house." Ever the diplomatic one. That was Stubbs. "Who's this woman?"

"That's Rosalita, our cook. Old man's her father; does chores. Boy's her son. Tends to the remuda. Jorge, or something like that."

Two of the hands rode up and sat their horses, looked down at the woman's body. None of them got off their horses.

"Vin. Hanson. I want you to see this." Kenedy nodded toward the cook's body.

"Woman could make some damn fine tortillas," said the one he'd called Hanson. He spat to his side. "Helluva hand with beans too."

Jobe blinked for a second, then stared at the man Kenedy had called Vin, who stared back at him, eyes narrowing. Dust half covered the faded light blue shirt Vin wore.

"Who would do this?" Stubbs asked.

"I have a fair to middling idea. What's your notion?" Kenedy's eyes narrowed.

"I don't have one. There's not a hoofprint in the area."

"What's that you're holding in your hand?" Kenedy leaned forward on his horse for a better look.

Stubbs started to hide it behind his back, then held it out, the branding iron with the Bentley brand on it.

"Where'd you find that?"

"It's what was used to kill the boy. Beat his head in."

"That's what I figured. Way I figured it all along," He turned to the one he'd called Vin. "Tell those boys to let them cattle go. We can round them up again, later. We're going to ride."

"You tell them. I'm not hired on to run your dern errands."

"You'll do what I say, when I say it."

"I doubt that."

Kenedy's face turned a near burgundy. He turned to Hanson. "You go tell them."

Hanson rode off.

"Just a minute, before you ride off half-cocked." Stubbs turned to Jobe. "You have any ideas on this now, Jenkins?"

Jobe hesitated. Then he shrugged.

"I think it was the Indian, Bent Feather. Covered up his tracks real fine, but he slaughtered a calf over yonder." Jobe nodded toward where they could still look and see buzzards circling.

"Bull feathers," Kenedy snapped. "It was Bentley, as sure as I'm sitting here wasting time flapping my gums with you when we could be riding."

He started to turn his horse.

"Just a minute." But Stubbs was talking to the wind. Kenedy took off at a gallop to get his men. Vin followed at a slower trot. He looked back at Jobe one last time, their gazes locked, then he rode off.

In a matter of moments they had all gathered around and had started off as full of business as any bunch like that can get.

Jobe had a good idea where they'd be heading, but it would be a tough job persuading them otherwise.

"Jenkins," Stubbs snapped. "Get a crew and bury the dead. Leastwise we can do that."

"Just a second, Sergeant."

"What?"

"Did you get a good gander at that fellow Vin?"

"Not in particular. Why?"

"He's that same fellow we helped get to town after the stage robbery. He was dressed as a preacher then. You recall?"

"You sure?"

"Yep. What do you think? He talked some right sass to Kenedy, and the old man sat there and took it."

"I never thought that fellow was no dern preacher then. No reason to start thinking so now."

CHAPTER EIGHTEEN

Justin went about his chores of weeding, feeding the goats, and harvesting what was fit to eat or sell at Aunt Sara's, letting himself become a part of the routine. It felt good. Even mucking out the horse stall with a pitchfork and tossing in fresh straw. He felt useful and a part of something for the first time in quite a while.

Every once in a while he caught a sideways glance from Button. She shared an occasional frown, or what he thought might even be a curled lip. She let her long red hair hang free now, hadn't covered it again with a blue bandanna. But she had reverted to her blue coveralls over a fading red shirt. They were all just workers now making the small ranch happen. Still, she was far too round-cheeked pretty to never smile. And those hazel eyes could throw a spark or two. Something was sure enough in her craw, though, and he lacked the experience to have any idea what that might be.

He came out of the house, blinking in the sun after the dim interior inside. He saw Francis hitching up the buggy.

"Where are you going?"

"Thought I'd take in this buggy and switch it out for a riding horse. Want to go along?"

Justin glanced back at the house. Button stood in the doorway staring at him. When she saw him looking she spun and stalked off toward the vegetable patch.

"What do you suppose is the matter with her?" Justin shook his head.

"Don't you know?"

"No. Not an earthly idea."

"Well, mull on it some. One minute you're all goggle-eyed every time she enters a room. Ever since you got biffed a good one, you're not."

"But she wasn't interested in me."

"She wasn't? She sure seems miffed enough at you for not paying as much attention to her as you were."

"But she . . . Oh, it's no use. I'll never understand women."

"That's the first intelligent thing you've said in a spell. Don't feel bad. No one does. At least I sure never have." He tightened the tack. "Now, you coming along?"

"Let me just tell Aunt Sara."

In a moment he came running back out of the house and climbed on beside Francis. He didn't share with him what his Aunt Sara had said, that it wouldn't break her heart if Justin came back alone. Francis grinned at him, gave a cluck, jiggled the reins, and they were off.

"I have a couple of former Ranger horses I could ready up for you," Sid said.

Justin thought he sensed something crafty in the way the liveryman said it, like he was pulling one over on them.

Francis didn't seem to notice. "Fine. I'll be right back, Justin. I'm just down the street for a moment."

Justin knew what that meant. He watched Francis walk all the way down to the saloon and then go inside.

Sid led a couple horses out front where Justin waited, tied them to the rail. One horse looked to be a big Tennessee Walker, brown with a white blaze down its nose and three white socks. The other was mostly black with a small white diamond down at the end of her nose.

Justin liked the smaller dark horse right away. "Why's she limp?"

"That's not a limp. She'll work that out after a short ride."

"It sure looks like a limp." Justin moved closer and looked at her left front leg. "Why did the Rangers get rid of these two?"

"Truth is, both these horses was snakebit. It's why the Rangers traded them in. But they're good sturdy horses. You can count on Rangers to pick out the like. Bein' snakebit's something a horse can get over, given time. I gave your friend there a right good rate on these." He could see the way Justin looked at the black horse. "Her name's Teddy."

"Teddy?"

"I guess someone didn't check until it was too late. That or it didn't matter nohow."

Justin saw Francis coming back up the street. His hands were empty and his face twisted into a scowl. "Let's go," he said as soon as he got to the horses. Without asking, he climbed up onto the bigger Tennessee Walker. "Coming?"

Justin shrugged and swung himself up onto Teddy.

The horse Francis rode showed off its flashy four-beat running walk. Justin's horse, Teddy, had a slight wobble as she trotted along to keep up.

They'd gone only about half the distance back to Sara's ranch when Francis looked back and saw Justin was falling farther behind. He sat his horse and waited until Justin caught up.

"Can't you keep up?"

"I might, but this horse can't. I tried to tell you back there. It's getting over being snakebit."

"I suppose we could rest the horses a mite before we go on." He nodded toward a stand of cottonwoods along a small creek. Dark shadowed patches showed on the ground. It would be cool there.

So it proved.

Justin led limping Teddy down to where the stream took a turn at the base of a sycamore and had formed a pool eight feet wide. He let her have a drink and then tied her where she could feed on some handy bunchgrass and rest her leg.

"I wish you'd let me know you'd pick the only three-legged horse in the place. I'd have picked up some liniment and maybe a crutch."

"Her name is Teddy," Justin said. He sat down so his back was to a tree. He left a nice tuffet of grass that formed a sort of throne chair for Francis. "That liveryman, Sid, told me the name of your horse is Boots."

"Oh."

"For a man whose publisher sent him out here to gather details, sometimes you skip over one or two."

"Oh, you're going to lecture me now on how I make my livelihood, are you?"

"No. I guess not, anyway. It's not what I intended. I just wish sometimes I had someone who wanted to make sure I was always on the right track. Someone who maybe could teach me how to draw and shoot a gun, maybe help me practice with it, so I could get by out here."

"I hear you. You miss your daddy."

"No I don't. Well, maybe I do. Such as he was. I sure didn't learn much from him. Maybe he had a thing or two left to teach. I won't know now." Justin stared at the creek, watched a water skipper shoot out from the shallows, sit for a second in the middle of a still spot among the ripples, then get swept down in the current until it disappeared out of sight.

"Well, I'm not your daddy, nor do I harbor any intentions of being so."

"I didn't think that."

"Good."

"You're just in a foul mood because you weren't able to buy any wine there in town. Well, the change will do you good."

"Hmpf."

Francis sat in a slump staring at the stream as well, maybe seeing something different from what Justin saw there. After a moment or two he straightened up. "What makes you say that?"

Justin hesitated. "Well, to tell you the truth, you're a bit of an ass when you drink."

"Do tell. Your observation?"

"Not my words. Aunt Sara's."

"Oh. She thinks that, does she?"

"Well, to be fair, everyone does. Scamp, Button, and maybe Missy too for all I can tell."

"And do you think that as well?"

"Of course." Justin didn't hesitate that time. Maybe he should have.

"I'm glad we had this little enlightening talk."

"See, you're still grumpy. Turns out you're no bargain sober either."

Francis stood up. For a second Justin thought he would mount up and ride away. Instead he took a step or two each way as he paced, then lowered himself to his tuffet again and looked directly at Justin.

"What kind of things do you think a good father would have told you? I mean one with your best interest at heart."

"I don't know. Maybe how to understand things better."

"Like what?"

"Why I did something that hurt, but felt good at the same time, and I did it for others, not myself, but it just makes some people . . ."

"Like Button?"

"Yeah, her. Not like me. Why?"

"Okay. Let's see here. If you did the thing for a noble cause, caring for her and the others more than yourself, then it shouldn't matter a whit what they think of you after."

"What?"

"It's just the way it is."

"Why?"

"Because that's how the mechanics of true heroism works. Didn't you know that?"

"No. And I still don't understand."

"You see, everyone can be a hero, of sorts. It's all about doing what you can, when you can."

"I still don't . . ."

Francis interrupted. "Let's say you're a cripple with a crutch, and you give that crutch away to someone who you see needs it more than you. Then that makes you a hero to the extent of your powers. You gave all you had to give, and had to make a sacrifice to do it."

"That's the kind of stuff you put in those books of yours?"

"Not exactly. But it's the same thing. In the books people are wanting high drama, shoot-outs at high noon, all that sort of thing. What you have to realize is that there are opportunities for heroics every day, if you see them and take advantage of them."

"I still don't understand."

"Fine. It'll give you something to mull over as we head back to the house. Now, what say we mount up and head in that direction?"

Justin nodded. When he swung up onto Teddy's back she seemed more rested and able to go, so they started off at a good pace toward his aunt Sara's place. Francis stayed silent most of the way, maybe mulling over a thing or two himself.

CHAPTER NINETEEN

Half the day ended up spent in wrong turns and heated arguments about which landmarks were being indicated on the map. Lucas watched the fevers growing to a near boil as the Bentley boys and their pa fussed and fumed over that stinking piece of paper. It was enough to make a cat laugh.

What a fine old southern family. Gabe, dark haired with a long rectangular face that flushed easily to red then burgundy, like his father. Esau, blond and what the ladies would find handsome. But, aside from his taste for women half his age, he had little to commend him as any kind of example. Any complexity he had came from being sly, clever to the point of being foxlike. Lucas could imagine he had spent his youth playing tricks and pranks on the slower moving. Now, to see them bickering the way they did, only made Lucas's heart feel good.

Still, by midday, the boys had floundered their way at last to the map's conclusion, the big X that marked the store of what they all expected to be a cache of Union gold. They pulled up their reins at a cemetery, a small family set of tombstones beside a cabin, of which remained only a blackened chimney rising out of a pile of aging ash. It's the way many families had turned out back when the federal troops had pulled out and left the settlers to fend for themselves.

One tombstone stuck out from the aging others made of limestone with inscriptions fading from years of exposure to rain, wind, and who knew what else out here in the middle of no damn where. This headstone was made of harder stuff, a round pink stone that had been polished smooth on one side where someone had painstakingly carved out: "You live all your life and find your treasure is in your heart."

"Someone sure as blazes spent more than a day carving out all that." Bentley turned to Lucas. "That's the spot already. You'd best get digging."

"You didn't hire me to do any digging. You want a hole, you look to someone else." Lucas's right hand hung down across his holster.

"I paid for that gun, and that horse. Get digging."

"No. I . . . don't . . . dig holes." Lucas's eyes narrowed and he swept across the lot of them. The only one who looked half game and stupid enough was Gabe.

Bentley knew that too and turned to Gabe. "You make a hole happen, right here, and I don't care how you do it." He rode his horse off into the shade of a small grove of pecan trees. He sat his horse and stared.

Gabe looked around at the others, then at Lucas. He swallowed. "Okay, fellas. Find something to dig with."

Lucas sat out in the sun and watched for a spell, then drifted off to the other side, didn't want to share shade with Bentley. He had a hunch about this. It took several hours of sweaty labor by the others to prove him right. Aside from several blisters on the hands of the others from using limbs and bits of old hardened, charred boards as shovels, they had nothing but a large and very empty hole, not even a casket.

"Damn those people. Damn them to hell." Captain Bentley stared down into the hole while the others remounted.

"Let's go," he said.

They all rode at a flat-out gallop, headed back for Sara Bolger's place. Lucas could feel the wind pressing at his face and tugging at his hat, pressing his shirt against him. He could feel his horse's lunging strides, hear its deep breathing, and see the foam begin to form on its neck. But he felt no joy from the ride. None at all.

Kenedy rode up at the front of his men, his face twisted in anger, not that someone had harmed his family, but that they had killed his servants, burned a building, and, worse, insulted him.

Vin, the Vinegar Kid, could see the rage bubbling at the surface. Even when they slowed to let the horses blow and catch their breath, Kenedy's face stayed flushed within the shadow of his hat's brim.

He turned to Vin. "You."

"What?" Vin's head turned slowly to Kenedy.

Kenedy's other hired men all looked toward the two of them.

"You have given me no end of sass. I want to know if you're worth putting up with."

"What do you have in mind?"

"I'd like to see you draw, to see if you're as blamed fast as they say."

Vin shrugged. "Who's fastest of your hired ones here? And who wouldn't you mind losing, if it comes to that?"

"Hanson there is no slouch."

Hanson's face washed a sudden pale gray.

"Anyone want to volunteer to go instead of Hanson?" Kenedy snapped.

The others looked away, many at the ground, which suddenly seemed to contain the most interesting dirt they'd ever seen.

"Hanson it is," Kenedy said.

"Okay." Vin looked Hanson over. "What kind of feather is that in your hat?"

"B . . . b . . . buzzard. I thought it was eagle, but the others put me right. I left it there because . . . well . . ." His words trailed off.

Kenedy and the others all moved off to one side, left Vin and Hanson both still on their horse facing each other.

"You sure we need to do this?" Hanson looked to Kenedy.

"Get it over with," he snapped.

"You feel up to this?" Vin said in a voice low enough that Hanson had to strain to hear it.

Hanson nodded, loosened his gun in its holster, and lifted his hand, but kept it close.

Vin drew, fired, and had his gun going back into its holster just as Hanson's hand touched the butt of his pistol.

Hanson's eyes opened wide. He slowly reached up, took off his hat, and looked at the stub of feather, all that remained of it.

"Thanks," he said, "for not killing me."

Vin nodded and turned to Kenedy. Kenedy was a very hard person to impress, and one who studiously avoided showing any emotion. But for just a flicker there, one eyebrow rose higher than usual.

"Okay, then," Kenedy said. "Just remember who's paying you."

Chapter Twenty

As they were coming up the last stretch of the lane to Sara Bolger's place, Justin's horse Teddy began to limp again, so he slowed, and Francis hung back with him. Neither said anything. They'd had a quiet ride with much for both of them to think about. Justin liked the way that seeing the Bolger place felt right away like home this time. He doubted Francis experienced a similar feeling.

There stood Scamp, over in the vegetable patch, working side-by-side with Button. Smoke curled out of the fort's chimney, so Sara must be inside with Missy cooking up some lunch. The sky looked sunny and bright, but Justin welcomed going inside to share food with everyone. He didn't let the annoying sound of thunder worry him at first, until he thought again about that clear sky.

He looked behind them, saw a billowing cloud of dust. It rumbled toward them. He and Francis both picked up their pace, rushed their horses to the shed and tied them, still with the saddles on. They ran to the house.

Button rushed past, dashed inside, and came back out as quickly carrying the shotgun. She hurried to the back to get up on the roof.

Sara wiped her hands on her apron and reached for her Winchester as they came inside.

"What can we do?" Justin shouted.

Missy made a noise from behind the drawn cloth that covered Sara's bed.

"You can keep your voices down until we're outside, for a start." Sara rushed past them to stand just inside the doorway.

Scamp came tearing through and grabbed the muzzle loader. He got into position at the open front window with the gun's barrel pointing out at the sound of approaching hooves.

The Bentley horde came charging up the lane. They didn't pull in until they were just a few feet away from Sara, who raised the Winchester. Justin was pretty sure she had a bead on the middle button on Captain Bentley's shirt.

"Hold it right there!" she yelled.

"Your map was no darn good." Bentley was still panting from the hard ride.

"I never said it was."

"You let me believe it was."

"I let you believe what you would. Don't lay that on me."

"I want the money, or I let Esau take the girl. We still have the papers for that."

"Your boys will have to serve them, because you'll be deader than Aaron Burr."

"What do you mean the map was no good? It looked just fine to me." The voice that boomed beside Justin came from Francis.

"You tell him." Bentley turned to Lucas. "You'll do that much, won't you?"

"It led them to a cemetery. A tombstone there read: 'You live all your life and find your treasure is in your heart.' The carving looked right, and was skilled, the way I hear everything else Justin's uncle Roger did. But the grave was empty."

"Empty, you say." Francis stood there, rubbing his chin, ignoring everyone else around him. Justin could just about hear the large brain working inside of that lunk of a head.

"I want to know what you're going to do about it." Bentley's voice grew even more stentorian. This was clearly something he felt quite strongly about, money.

Francis held up a hand. "Quiet. I'm thinking."

"Will someone shoot this man for me?" Bentley turned to the men behind him.

Several drew pistols or their carbines.

"Oh, for heaven's sake," Francis said. "It's clear you want something or you're going to do some harm here. I don't want anyone here to get hurt. Give me just a second or two to parse this out. I can hardly think for all the clatter."

Bentley looked to Lucas, who shrugged. The other men looked to Bentley, who held up a hand.

"I hope you come up with something, Mr. Francis." Sara kept her voice low and firm. "Because we're quite up against it here. At the very least, old Captain Bentley's going down, if I have any say in this."

Francis's head came up in a snap. He smiled.

"What?" Sara said.

"What?" Bentley repeated.

Francis turned to Sara. "Your brother-in-law Roger, he was the handyman around here, wasn't he?"

"Yes. You already know that."

"Probably was his work on the tombstone. Of course no one was buried there."

"What the devil are you going on about?" Bentley spoke between clenched teeth.

Justin didn't know when he'd seen someone more ready to snap.

"Don't you see?" Francis waved a hand toward the fort. "This place was an abandoned fort when the family moved here. Roger Bodean did most of the fixing up. He was handy with wood, and he was handy with stone. Do you see? He built the hearth.

135

Now do you get it?"

"It's in the hearth," Lucas yelled. "Now I see it. 'Your treasure is in your heart.' Your *hearth*. It's the way a clue map should work."

"Someone get a pickax." Bentley climbed down from his horse. The men behind him lowered their long guns and slid pistols back into holsters.

Sara lowered her Winchester. "Give me a moment to get the children and the soup out of there. Then you can do what you will."

Justin could see that it was the only rational answer, unless they all wanted to go out in a blaze of gunfire. He sure hoped there was something in that danged hearth.

Sara carried Missy out of the fort. Scamp came out carrying the muzzle loader and the small cauldron holding the soup. It was like Sara to worry about her family's next meal, even when they were perched right on the very edge of their existence.

Esau came back from the goat shed carrying a pickax. He and half a dozen of Bentley's men pushed inside. Justin managed to slip in and press back against the wall, just inside the door. He wanted to be able to yell for the others to run if this turned out to be another bust.

Gabe grabbed the pickax and began to flail away at the middle of the hearth. Chips of rock went flying, and so did sparks sometimes when the pick blade struck a small bit of flint.

Esau and a couple of the others pulled rocks away as they were loosened.

"There! There it is," Bentley shouted. He pointed, and the men reached in, started pulling out leather sacks with a US stamp on them. Bentley grabbed one of the bags, looked inside and didn't say a word. But his eyes glittered, and he came as close to smiling as Justin had ever seen.

"Gabe. You and Esau load this into your saddle bags and

mine. We're going home, boys."

Justin beat them outside then the whole lot came pouring out. They tucked all the bags onto their horses, mounted, and turned and started up the lane, never saying anything to Sara or even looking back.

"This isn't over, I fear," Sara said. She carried Missy back inside. Scamp brought in the pot of soup. She watched him set it down as she got a broom and started sweeping up what chips and rock dust as she could. "At least we can eat."

Justin and Scamp knelt down and started piling the loose rocks out of the way. Button came in, put away her shotgun and got another broom to help Sara.

"We can tend to that later, fix it up fine." Francis waved at the mess that had been the hearth. "I'll ride to town and get some mortar. How hard can that be? If Roger can do it, so can I. I just need to make sure I get the kind that's right for a fireplace."

"You're certainly helpful and obliging all of a sudden."

"The error of my ways has been tactfully pointed out to me."

"Oh." Sara tilted her head when she looked at him. "Well, for now we sit down and eat while the soup is still warm. Button, why don't you and Justin fetch out the plates."

Button went about it without looking at Justin. While helping, his hands bumped into hers and a shock went all the way through him that made his hair nearly stand on end. He set the plates he carried down onto the table, making a small clatter.

Aunt Sara looked at him. "Whatever is the matter with you?"

They settled in at the table. After all they'd been through, the act of eating together seemed to calm them, even though Justin had only to glance to his right to see where Bentley's bunch had torn the dickens out of the hearth and taken the money he'd hoped would save her farm. Still, they had their guns, the fort, and were being left alone for the moment, and out this way that was a lot to ask for and get in itself.

"After we eat, I'll ride to town," Francis said.

"You don't have to." Sara looked up at him, a spoon still poised halfway to her mouth.

"I want to."

"My. You two must have had some talk out there."

Francis kept his head down, eating. Scamp and Justin exchanged a glance.

"Are you sure you don't also want to have a look-see where those men went with that money?" She still held her spoon in midair.

"Well, I do think I'll ride after those men as well and see where they go. Maybe there's a way to get some of it back. Taking it all is just robbery."

"That what those men are," Sara said. "Robbers. Just plain robbers. Now, eat. Okay?"

"It's your money, the way I see it, Sara. If I can get the least bit of it back, it would help you out of your fix."

"You mean that, don't you?"

"Yes. Yes, I do. I don't need money. You do. Justin could ride along. Make sure I stay straight and true."

"You're set on this, aren't you?"

"It's time I did something for you."

"You mean that?" Her voice and face still showed doubt.

"At the very least I could round up that mortar while I'm at it."

"I'll go too, Aunt Sara." Justin felt better just saying it.

"I want to go," Scamp shouted.

"No. You stay."

"Why's Justin get to go?"

"He's old enough to make his own choices and decisions. You're not."

"Aw, Mom."

Justin sneaked a peek at Button. She looked down at her soup as if it were the most interesting soup she'd ever seen. But her cheeks turned a rosy pink.

Outside a thunder seemed to sound, though the sky had been clear when they came inside. Justin glanced toward the door. Scamp jumped up, rushed to it and looked outside.

"Rangers!" he shouted.

Francis leaned closer to Sara. "Maybe it'll be better if we don't tell them about the gold just yet. Chances are it's government property and they might just take it back."

She hesitated, then nodded.

CHAPTER TWENTY-ONE

Jobe and Bo rode at the front of the Rangers as they came up Sara Bolger's lane once again. When Captain Marberry rode out with the Frontier Battalion, he liked to ride up front himself, said he wouldn't put any of his men through anything he wouldn't face first. Stubbs was more of a rear-echelon man, didn't mind hanging back in case of ambush or other surprises.

Up ahead, Jobe saw the mother, Sara, just outside the front door holding her Winchester. One small figure came out the door with a shotgun and headed around back to get up on the roof. Another barrel stuck out the front window at the approaching Rangers. He watched Justin and Francis, who he felt he knew by now, come out and stand beside Sara.

Jobe and Bo reined in a few feet away.

"You don't have to go to battle positions when we ride up, ma'am." Jobe lifted his hat to her.

"I'm never sure out here," she said.

Jobe heard a click and looked up to the roof. A shotgun pointed back at him. The girl holding it looked ready to pull the trigger.

"What do you want?" Sara said.

"We've come to warn you that there's been an Indian attack near you, we think."

"You think?"

"It's a pretty clever bunch." Jobe started to say more, decided not.

Sergeant Stubbs and the others came up to fall in behind Jobe. Stubbs eased to the front, glanced around, taking in the situation. He seemed to be mulling over how much to share. Should they mention that the whole Kenedy bunch was running wild just now?

"Spread over there," Stubbs nodded in the direction of the Kenedy ranch house, "had three servants killed. Jenkins thinks it was the Comanche bunch. I didn't see any confirmation sign, but I'll willing to accept his word. You all might be in danger."

"We have been since we moved here," Sara said, "and have gotten by in spite of everything."

"Okay. Seems we rode all this way over to warn you for nothing."

"We appreciate it," Francis said. "Don't think we don't."

"I'll speak for myself, thank you very much." Sara glared up at him.

"It's fun to be feisty at times. All the same, it's a fine idea to be polite and appreciative now and again," Francis said.

Her mouth opened, then closed. She turned back to the Rangers.

"If that's all you have to say, well . . ." She stopped at the sound of more hooves pounding up the lane behind Stubbs's small troop of men. "Oh, my stars in heaven, now what?"

The Rangers behind him parted enough for Jobe to see up through them to what looked to be another Ranger troop riding up the lane. This one, though, had its officer up front—man in a wide slouch hat with three pheasant feathers sticking out of it. His clothes looked impeccable. The men behind him rode in twos, side by side with a precision Jobe had rarely seen outside of cavalry units.

Jobe glanced to Bo, who looked back with wide open eyes. That could be only one person: Ranger Lieutenant Cawley. Oh, he was a stickler. In his outfit, once his men were mounted, he would yell, "Fall in!" His men would fall into line in a company front. He'd yell, "Right dress." Heads would snap to the right, and the line would straighten. "Count off from left to right!" They'd do that. "Count off by twos." They'd respond. "Twos right. Forward . . . march!" And off they'd go riding in this two-by-two formation. Why, that sort of thing would have done in Jobe and the others in Stubbs's lot. But it looked like they were in for a taste of that for a spell.

Cawley reined in and held up the flat of his hand. "Halt!"

The line behind him came to a stop, kept the same order without moving.

"Saints in heaven," Bo whispered.

Cawley sat upright and stiff as a flagpole in his saddle. Though he wasn't allowed to wear either blue or gray, his buckskin shirt looked like it had been ironed onto him, and was as close to a uniform cut as could be. His hair flowed blond and long in the back, his beard trimmed on the sides and coming to a point below. His mustache had been trimmed into a thin line with points on either end. Jobe doubted if anyone ever looked more like a young blond Satan.

Jobe had heard that Cawley had been most particular about how he'd put together his troop. Although he had himself been born in Texas, he had gone out of his way to exclude Texans. He had mustered up men from about every state south of the Mason-Dixon Line, many from Virginia, others from Georgia, Mississippi, Alabama, and even one ruddy-face Scotsman. That way none of his men were likely to have kin or friends in Texas, and thus were unlikely to favor anyone.

"Sergeant Stubbs?" Cawley had a booming voice, one he seemed to enjoy using at its fullest volume.

"Right here." Stubbs turned his horse.

"Report, please. How are you coming along with that renegade Comanche bunch? Bent Feather, wasn't it?"

"We're . . . we're on his trail, sir."

"Where is he, then?"

"We don't rightly know, sir."

"Not much of a trail then, is it?"

"No, sir."

"And the stage robbers. Getting anywhere there?"

"No, sir." Stubbs glanced toward Jobe. He thought it best not to share half-developed notions.

"You haven't made very much progress here, have you?"

"We just came from the Kenedy spread. Persons unknown killed three of the servants while Kenedy and his men were away, possibly rustling."

"What have you done about that?"

"We buried the victims, sir."

"I see."

A silence settled over the group. Jobe thought it pretty low of Cawley to dress out Stubbs this way in front of everyone instead of in private when they were alone. But it was every bit the way he was.

"So, it seems you have very little to crow about, Sergeant."

"No one was crowing," Stubbs muttered. He kept his head erect and straight forward, but Jobe sensed a different posture inside the man.

"Well, be that as it may. We have fresh orders. You and your men are to come with me. Mexican desperadoes are kicking up all along the southern border and need our attention. Captain Marberry will join up with us down there, and we'll begin a full-scale cleanup. First, we head to town and get supplies, then head south. Can you get your men into some kind of order?"

Jobe and the others did the best they could to struggle into a line of twos, side by side, though it felt as unnatural to most of them as wearing their boots on the wrong feet. Stubbs rode beside Jobe. Bo and Zed were right behind. They kept their burro in the middle beside one of the men, the same as Cawley had his pack burro in his outfit.

Cawley turned his horse and rode back to the other end of the column. "Left . . . face. Left . . . face." With his men turned to face forward, Stubbs's men closed up behind them.

Cawley's voice seemed just as loud and assertive heard from the back of the column. "Forward . . . march!"

Jobe knew that they would be riding drag and eating dust all the way. It would be a small punitive slap for whatever. He loosened his neck scarf and lifted it up over his nose. He'd ride this way, but derned if he was going to die from eating dust while doing it.

As soon as the Rangers passed out of sight in the distance, Francis turned to Sara. "I'd best be off, see what I can do about finding where Bentley and his bunch went . . . and, of course, picking up some mortar. We'll have that hearth back in shape for you soon as we can."

"Sure you will."

Scamp ran off and came back with their still-saddled mounts. He might not be allowed to ride along, but he could do his bit. He grinned at Justin as he handed him Teddy's reins.

"Why don't you take one or two of the guns, just in case?" Sara said.

"I'd rather you kept them here. You still have a family to protect." Francis gave her a half grin, meant to look humble and brave at the same time.

"Are you saying you'd ride out into all that unarmed?" She waved a hand at the vast untamed land around them.

He dug in his pocket and came out with the small derringer he still carried in his pocket. "If they just come close enough, I'll let them see the measure of my wrath."

"You're as tomfool as anyone I ever met," she said, and nearly grinned for a second.

Francis swung himself up into his saddle, reached down to pat Boots on the side of his neck. "Don't worry. I'll put you next to something to eat first chance I get."

Justin put one foot in the near stirrup, ready to pull himself up into the saddle.

Button pushed loose from the wall where she was leaning and rushed to him, drew him close, and kissed him on the cheek. "Be careful."

She spun and scurried off inside.

Sara just shook her head.

Justin could feel his own cheeks flush red, but doubted they got any redder than Button's had been. He swung himself up into the saddle and they were off. Two of the sorriest adventurers the West ever saw. But if a kiss was any kind of fuel, Justin felt ready for a week or two of anything the West could throw at him.

Chapter Twenty-Two

Bentley eased his horse closer to Lucas. "You didn't think that map was any good, did you?"

"Nope," he admitted. He looked at Bentley, but the man wasn't smug or gloating, just looked like someone who was richer than he already had been and was deriving a great deal of satisfaction from that. Bentley spurred his horse and moved out to the front of his men.

The men had slowed to a mile-eating steady trot, were halfway to the Bentley spread.

Lucas kept an eye on every rise and mesa around them. Now that they were toting what was serious money out in these parts, he didn't trust anyone, much less the men he was riding with. But there were plenty of places between here and the Bentley spread where someone could lie in wait and bushwhack them. And Bentley had not gone about his business through the years spreading goodness and light to all he met. The man had more enemies than a rattlesnake. He'd earned them.

They rode out in the open, the way the Bentleys knew to be the shortest, straightest path back to their spread. Buffalo grass rose up above his horse's fetlocks, halfway to Old Top's knees. Occasional green dots of prickly pear cactus spotted the light brown grass. They avoided those. At the far edges of the open space the ground looked rumpled as a rug and rose to a mesa on one side and a higher crest of ground on the other. Perfect place for an ambush.

Around him the two Bentley boys and other hands were grinning as if they were all on their way to a barn dance. Suddenly, Captain Bentley reined in his horse so hard, he nearly launched himself clear off the saddle. A line of riders stretched out across their path.

Lucas looked behind their bunch. Riders peeled out from either side and came together to close off that end. Old Captain Bentley had been a military man. He'd know a maneuver when he saw one. Right now they were outflanked and outnumbered. Not a good spot. Not a good spot at all.

Lucas looked around. A rock pile ran along the base of the mesa and might have space to get some men and horses behind. Nothing promising in the other direction.

He rode up to the front where Gabe and Esau had already eased up to rein in beside their father.

"What do you want? We're just on our way home," Bentley shouted.

"I expect you are. But odds are you don't make it." Kenedy stood high in his stirrups to yell.

"What the devil are you talking about?"

"My ranch. You and your boys killed my servants."

"You're eating loco weed. None of my men were at your spread. We've been elsewhere."

"Where do you claim to have been? And you'd better have witnesses."

Lucas could see they were getting into a tight spot. If they admitted where they'd been, it might lead to others trying to take the gold from them. He could see Bentley mulling over his options hard. Lucas hoped he'd spotted the same cover over to their right, because Lucas was surely enough going to cut and go for that, given half a chance.

"I've an idea."

"What is it, you murderer?"

"I'm admitting nothing. We weren't at your place. But I see little way of convincing you otherwise."

"You're right about that."

"How about this? My best against your best."

Kenedy hesitated only a second. "Fair enough."

He might have Bentley's bunch outnumbered, but a bout of all-out shooting would take its toll on both sides, and it might just happen that one of those plugged was Kenedy himself. He had to know for a certain fact he was the top target most of them would be gunning for. This way was fair enough, and if he lost, he might just attack anyway. He seemed as mad as a yard full of wet hens.

Bentley turned to Lucas. "Well, it's about time you earn your pay at last."

"Pay I haven't gotten. What say you spare a bit of that gold before I go out to face whoever?"

Bentley's mouth tightened and his face clenched like a baby taking a dump in its diaper. He finally relaxed enough to reach into his saddlebag, fetch a handful of gold coins out, and hold it out.

Lucas rode close, took the handful and shoved the gold into his pocket. "Okay, then."

He turned and rode out to the middle of the space. Vin, the Vinegar Kid, rode out from the other side, facing him.

They stopped in the middle, sat facing each other.

"Been a spell," Lucas said.

"Not long enough." Vin grinned.

"How you been keeping?"

"Can't complain."

"Well, I suppose we should get this rodeo started."

"Okay by me."

CHAPTER TWENTY-THREE

Francis set a reasonable pace, deferring to Justin's horse Teddy. So far she hadn't been limping. But riding any harder than they were might quickly enough do her in.

Just as well. Justin bobbed up and down and a little side to side. He had not ridden much back east and his backside was starting to feel a little bruised and sensitive. He wasn't alone, if the winces Francis sometime showed meant anything.

Still, he had never felt more alive. The sky looked a clear pale blue with wisps of clouds feathered in streaks along the horizons. The wind swayed the tops of the tall brown grass in waves. Trees formed a line along a creek far off to their left. And no one had shot at them or even pointed a gun their way, and they'd been out on the Bentleys' trail for well over two hours.

Francis slowed down. "Do you know anything about reading sign on trails?"

"Not really." Justin rode up to look down where Francis was pointing.

"You see, this one set of prints, the Bentley bunch, is moseying along the way we're following. Then this other set of prints comes along and is on top of the first set."

"Someone's following them? Is right on their tail?"

"That's the way I'd read it. But who? Those Rangers?"

"There's enough new prints for that. But you saw those men. They were riding side-by-side in twos." Justin glanced ahead, saw nothing.

"Says something about their leader being a little too prim and proper to be in the middle from what I've seen so far."

"Maybe he has a strong military background. But I'll bet all of those Rangers are scrappy enough in a fight." Justin stared down at the prints. "Those Rangers, though, are headed for town. These prints all aim for the Bentley spread."

"You're probably right. You're also probably right that this is no Ranger bunch. But another thing is bothering me too."

"What's that?"

"I see occasional sign of an unshod horse or two."

"Indians?"

"I can only guess. Though it doesn't make sense."

"I haven't seen any Indians." Justin looked around to their sides.

"I don't believe you're supposed to. They're just suddenly there giving you the haircut of a lifetime."

"What do you think we should do?"

"Can you get a little more pep out of old Teddy there? If you can, I think we should ride harder, see if we can catch up and make any sense of this."

"I'll sure try." He reached forward to pat Teddy on the withers. "How about you?"

She shook her head. Maybe she understood more than she let on. But he dug in his heels and she spurted into a faster trot to keep up with Francis on Boots.

Teddy was holding up better than Justin expected. Ahead of him, Francis held up a hand and pointed right. As soon as he turned and started veering off in that direction, Justin could make out in the distance a line of men on horseback facing the other direction. They seemed to be blocking this end of the piece of valley ahead.

Francis led them to the backside of the mesa, where it sloped upward to the top. "Let's leave the horses here." A row of low shrubs and the beginning of what in time would be a stand of mesquite trees lined the bottom of the slope. Francis tied his horse to a limb, with enough slack for him to reach some bunch-grass below. Justin did the same with Teddy.

They scrambled through the brambles of vegetation that tugged at their pants legs and made their way up the slope as fast as they could go. Justin got to the top first and heard the rasp of Francis's panting as he caught up. Once he got to the top as well, he bent to hold his knees for just a moment to catch his breath.

"Come on," Justin whispered. He headed over toward the other edge of the mesa, where the table dropped down in a straight edge to the valley below.

He looked around. The best spot for watching seemed to be a ridge of rocks that went up to the trunk of a young live oak tree that still cast a shadow. Justin crouched down there. Francis came up beside him, scooted close to look over, too. His breath still came in raspy gulps that slowed as he settled into place.

Below, Justin could see the Bentley men in the middle, with men sealing off either end of the valley.

"Those are Kenedy's men." Francis pointed. "We saw them when they came to the ranch earlier."

"I don't see any Indians."

"Nor do I."

"Then what did those tracks you spotted mean?"

"I don't have an earthly idea. I only know what I'm seeing before me right now."

"Sure are a lot of them."

"Enough to pry gold loose from Bentley? I guess we'll see. This could go a couple of different directions. We might get some kind of opportunity yet."

"What's going on now?" Justin nearly stood up. Francis pulled him back down behind the cover of the rocky ridge.

"Seems like one man from each group is heading out to the middle. Maybe some kind of showdown. One from each side going to shoot it out. I've heard of such things."

"One of them is Lucas," Justin said. "You recall that buckskin vest he wore. And the other is the preacher, except he's got on a different shirt."

"Your eyes are better than mine. But I suspect that man is no kind of preacher."

"Two hired guns, then? One from each side?"

"That's the way it looks to me, Justin. Oh, that's right clever of Bentley. Look how he's pulling his men to one side, so they don't get in the way of the shoot-out. But he's moved them all closer to that pile of rocks under us that runs along the bottom of this mesa. If they get half a chance I'm betting they dash for cover behind those rocks. It's their only chance, since there are more men in Kenedy's bunch."

Justin watched the two lone riders come together in the middle. They seemed awfully close to each other. Both could wind up dead. They seemed to be talking. Perhaps the usual back-and-forth before bullets flew. Justin realized he was chewing the inside of his cheek to keep from yelling out. He knew he was about to see a man die, and he'd known them both.

"Taking a good while to get at it," Francis muttered.

The delay had given Bentley and his men opportunity to ease back even closer to the rocky cover along the mesa's bottom.

Any second now, Justin thought. He grew tense.

Tick.

Tick.

Any second.

Tick.

Then both riders in the middle turned and rode off together, side by side. The men on the far side parted and let them through, no one wanting to open fire on the two fastest men out there.

Justin could hear Kenedy shouting from the far right. "Come back here, you two. I'm paying you both."

"How can that be?" Justin whispered.

"Looks like Kenedy's little fix in the situation just came undone. He must have hired Lucas to ride with Bentley's bunch as well as that so-called preacher to ride with his lot. I'll bet he didn't plan on it coming down to this. Even so, I suspect he thought he'd kept the fastest one of them for his side. Lucas must be the one who got that telegram I got a peek at before you picked it up about ruining a man, and maybe hadn't gotten around to tripping Bentley up just yet."

"Seems a complex way of going about it."

"Oh, what a tangled web we weave."

"Who?"

"Kenedy, looks like."

"But why did they leave together like that?"

"You know, Justin, I have a sneaking suspicion that if you were to ask the two of them about that they might fess up to being brothers."

"Brothers?"

"That or darned good friends. That's the way I see it, and the only way to make what I just saw as much as a pickled onion of sense. Rotten luck for Kenedy, all the same."

In the short time it took for the two gunslingers to get through Kenedy's men on the far side and ride away, all of Bentley's bunch rushed flat out for the cover and had slipped behind the rocks with their horses by the time Kenedy's men on either side started to close in on them, firing away as they came.

Bullets slammed into the dirt, pinged off the side of the mesa and ricocheted off rocks. Dirt and chips went flying everywhere.

Bullets poured back at the attacking men from behind the rocks. Justin saw one man fly backward off his horse and two other horses collapse, riders and all.

Kenedy's men soon hit the dirt and crawled forward, shooting away. A few of the horses scampered away.

"Charge them! Charge them!" Kenedy screamed. But none of his men seemed inclined to do what he asked: rush foolhardily into a flurry of bullets.

Instead, they eased steadily closer in a tightening ring around the Bentley bunch. The horses there weren't safe either. Justin heard them whinny and one scream in pain the way only a horse can.

"What do we do?" Justin crouched low, as if the bullets were coming right at him instead of making the incredible racket below.

"Do? Why, we wait. We might just get our hands on that gold again yet. I doubt if Kenedy even knows about that . . . yet."

"What if Bentley tells him, and tries to buy his way out of this with it?"

"I doubt he even tries. A man as mad as this Kenedy seems to be is in no state to dicker with."

The shooting continued back and forth, sporadic, now and again in a flurry of shots. Justin couldn't tell who was getting any kind of advantage. He couldn't see much of Bentley's men below, but he could make out quite a few of Kenedy's scattered in an ever-widening half circle on the ground as they took cover where they could.

"I wish I had a watch," Francis said. He and Justin lay there as the shots kept going back and forth into the afternoon.

"Why?"

"So I could tell if those two slingers met at high noon."

"Why does that matter? They both rode away together without firing a shot at each other."

"It would just be interesting to me. That's all."

A wayward shot ricocheted high off the lip of the mesa. Justin ducked low again, hugged rock. "You think we'll make it out of this?"

"We're not at risk way up here. All the shooting is down there."

Justin heard a rustle coming behind them. Someone was coming up over the edge of the Mesa very near to where they lay.

He got slowly to his feet and stared in that direction, looking carefully about. A head popped up from over the edge and looked right at him. Justin took a step back.

Bentley's son Esau came scrambling over the top and rushed toward him.

"Francis!" Justin called out.

"Hold it right there."

Esau whirled, saw Francis standing there, arm extended with the tiny derringer nearly lost in his giant fist.

"You must be kidding me." Esau raised his gun.

There was no time to think, so Justin just dove, slamming into the back of Esau's knees. The knees buckled as he fired.

Francis rushed from the other direction, catching Esau once again on the side of his head with his left fist.

Esau collapsed like the Roman Empire into a pile of loose arms and legs.

Justin dusted himself as he got back to his feet. "Thanks. Are you okay?"

"No. But thank you all the same. I believe he would have plugged me worse if you hadn't distracted him. I do think he winged me a bit."

Blood oozed from a hole in Francis's shirt just under and inside his right shoulder.

"Must've been aiming for the heart." Francis put his other

hand over the wound, plopped slowly down onto a rock for a seat.

"We've got to get help for you."

"How? What's your plan for that?"

"Look." Justin pulled his shirttail out and tore off a long strip. "Let me try to patch you for now. Stop the blood flow."

"That the best you can do?"

"Well, I could apply a tourniquet at the neck."

Francis's head snapped toward him. "I wouldn't have credited you with a wry sense of humor."

"I wouldn't have credited you with getting shot just when we should be getting out of here."

"Touché."

"What?"

"Just leave me here in loose rocks. I'll be fine."

"No. I'm taking you down to the horses, get you to someone who knows how to patch you up right. Now, hold still. Can you lift your shirt up?"

Francis tried, but his face twisted in pain. Moving the one arm came hard for him.

"Let me help." Justin tugged the shirt up until he could see the hole that went in at the front, might have grazed the outside of a rib, and had come out the back as a bigger hole. If Justin had been hit in the same place by a bullet of that caliber, it would have probably knocked him unconscious and perhaps sent him into shock. He was going to need more cloth.

He tore two long strips from the bottom of Francis's shirt, and only as he was ripping off the last one did it occur to him that these were the only shirts they had. By tying the strips together at the ends he had a strip long enough to wrap all the way around Francis's barrel of a chest. He pulled it as tight as he could so it covered and pressed against the wounds on both sides. Then he tied a couple of knots on the far side from the wounds. Blood was already starting to seep through, but the makeshift bandage would slow the bleeding and maybe let the wounds clot. It's all he knew to do, or could do for now.

Francis helped as Justin tugged the shirt back into place, what was left of it. A wide strip of Francis was left bare all the way around his waist, hairy, and a good part of it belly.

"I look a right tomfool, don't I?"

"Won't be the first time," Justin muttered.

"What?"

"Let's just get you down the hill. Okay? But first, I better take a look at Esau. You hit him pretty hard."

"If he's still out, bong him on the head a couple of times with his own revolver. You owe him that much."

Justin went over and bent closer to Esau, who had crumpled to the ground. His arms and legs twisted this way and that as if he'd fallen from the sky. Justin got closer, could see Esau's chest rising and falling. He was alive, but as out of it as a dead mackerel.

"I suppose he was either on a flanking maneuver to get out and around on the other side of Kenedy's bunch," Francis said, "or he was thinking of cutting out in a run away from here on his own."

"Either makes sense," Justin agreed.

"Fetch me his peashooter while you're at it." Francis sat awkwardly on his rock, favoring his hurt right side. "And a handful of shells out of his belt."

Justin picked up the gun from where it lay on the ground after falling out of Esau's limp hand. Looked the same as the Colt Peacemaker he'd seen Lucas buy back at the general store. Heavy gun for his hand. He imagined it smacking down on his head, could still feel a twinge from that. For a second he considered Francis's suggestion that he pop Esau a couple of times on the head as payback. But that sort of thing wasn't in him. So he thumbed a dozen extra bullets out of Esau's gun belt and brought the pistol and bullets over to Francis. He shoved the revolver into his belt and the shells into a side pocket.

"Ah, I feel better about our chances now."

"Yeah. I don't think that fancy lady's little gun was doing us much good."

"All the same." Francis dug the little gun out of his other pants pocket, opened it, saw he hadn't fired it, that it was still loaded. He closed it and shoved it back into his pocket.

"You're going to have to help me here," Justin said. He started to try to tug Francis upright.

"I can get my own darned self up. There's nothing wrong with my legs or my other wing."

Francis pushed himself up off the rock with his good hand, wobbled only a tiny bit. There was nothing casual about getting hit with a bullet like that.

"Okay. Let's get down to those horses."

Easier said than done. Though they had charged pretty briskly up the slope to get to the top of the mesa, getting down was another matter.

Justin found himself picking each step with care, and the task seemed even more daunting to Francis. Each step seemed to jolt all the way up to his wound. He winced often, but at least kept any sounds down to muffled groans.

Shots came steadily from the back-and-forth going on in the valley on the other side of the mesa, sometimes a steady barrage, others times single calculated shots. It was no place to be, and Justin was happy to be on the other side of the hill.

"Bunch of tomfools," Francis muttered. "Helluva thing to fight and feud like that. Won't be enough left on either side to enjoy anything like spoils."

Justin thought Francis was going to take a tumble down the hill once. Francis's boot heels slid on sand and gravel, but he caught himself and straightened until he was upright again. It would have been a long roll to the bottom, and cactus and thorny scrub bushes were between where they were and the bottom.

Justin kept an eye on Francis and watched for snakes as well. This whole area looked snaky as the dickens, and he wouldn't have been surprised to hear a rattler's warning at any second.

The last bit was hardest. Rocks were piled loose in the scree that had rolled down the hill through the years. They'd scampered across it fine going up, but while they came down, each rock seemed to twist and turn under foot, have a mind of its own, ready to sprain an ankle or send them tumbling.

Justin breathed a deep sigh when they finally got to the bottom. Francis straightened and looked about.

As soon as they worked their way around to where they'd left the horses, Justin could see that only one of them was there. Teddy. Boots was nowhere to be seen.

"Well, now. Isn't that just a buffalo chip." Francis kicked at a low agarita bush.

Justin would have agreed, but he was busy examining where Francis had tied the reins. The limb was twisted and broken. But some Comanche could have done that as readily as Boots jerking free to get at more grass. He looked around on the ground, but saw no footprints.

"That puts us in a right pickle," Francis said.

"Well, Teddy can't carry you, especially you and me both," Justin said. "She can barely handle me."

"I wish I could disagree, but I can't."

Justin looked around. "Will you be all right hiding somewhere here if I go for help?"

"Where do you intend to go? The town's a ways from here."

"Those Rangers were on their way to it. Maybe I can head them off and get them to come this way. They're always looking about for something peppery to get in the middle of, and I suppose this qualifies as much as anything."

Shots still sounded from the other side of the mesa. From here they seemed more distant, subdued, but no less deadly. Some of those men were wrapping up their days over there, and it made Justin glad to be far from them. Lucas and that so-called preacher'd had the right idea when they had cut out of there.

Francis frowned as he looked around. "I guess I'll just hunker down in the shade of these stickers. No one will look for me there."

"Good idea."

"I was joshing."

"I wasn't. I have to go, and now." Justin waited until Francis had scooted back into the shadows of the low scrub bushes. Big as he was, he disappeared the way a small spotted fawn does in the low shadows. Good.

"Hey." The voice came out of the shadows. "You should take Esau's pistol."

"You're apt to need it more than me. I'd probably drop it in all the blazing speed I intend to make on Teddy here."

Justin untied her, swung up into the saddle, turned and headed toward where he thought he might angle to catch up with the Rangers.

"Give it your best, Teddy." And they were off.

Francis lay in shade that wasn't all that cool. The breeze seemed to sweep around the spot where he hid. He listened to the click of Teddy's hooves as Justin rode away, slow at first, then breaking into a trot, from there to a gallop as the sounds faded in the distance. He was alone.

Every now and then he thought he heard something, usually imagined. But a rustle of leaves did snap his head left. He

expected snake, instead saw a lizard running across the leaf litter, left front leg going forward at the same time as the right
back leg. It came to a stop barely a foot from his face, did slow
push-ups as it considered him. Its throat rose out below in a red
arch, snapped back, rose out again. Then it made up its mind,
spun, and took off with its antic alternate running, tail whipping back and forth as it ran.

He half dozed as he lay there, a patina of sweat forming on
his forehead. His wounds throbbed, but they seemed to be scab-
bing over in their own healing way if he didn't move. After what
seemed hours, he heard approaching sounds. Low hoof clicks
tapped the ground, coming his way. At first he thought they
were far away, then he realized they weren't the sounds of a
shod horse. A Comanche was coming his way. He stayed as still
as he could. Hardly breathed at all. He could see them now,
from hoof to pastern, the legs of the paint horse were covered
with something. Now, so close he thought he could reach out to
them, he could see the covering was a rawhide sock tied into
place over each hoof. He'd heard about this before, something
Apaches did to sneak up quietly and to leave no prints. Maybe
it was something Bent Feather picked up at the reservation.
Mighty clever of him. Still, it felt an hour now since Francis had
taken a breath.

The hooves kept moving, and the eyes of the rider must have
been sweeping the slope, not looking down to the bottom
shadows beneath the bushes.

When the hooves had moved on and their soft sound had
faded, Francis breathed out and then took a huge gulping swal-
low of air. It was the closest he had come to being a bad toupee
hanging from an Indian's waist since they'd been staked out
naked in the sun.

Sure enough he had come out to the west to gather detail
and color, but he would have far preferred taking his notes from

some more peaceful place farther away from the serious action and risk than this. He let out another long breath. Whew.

CHAPTER TWENTY-FOUR

Teddy held up just fine for the first few miles, then Justin began to detect a hitch that was growing into a limp. Not good. He had only a fair idea of where the Rangers would be by now, and he wasn't as close as he'd like to be.

Being on his own out here, riding flat out on a mission to save someone, made him think of pony express riders. They had often ridden through a hail of arrows or bullets, from what he'd read, and most had lived to tell the tale. Maybe he'd even read of their adventures in one of those dime novels Ben Blunt wrote. Nice to think he was living an adventure as fine, though he could do without the arrows and bullets.

He was feeling quite full of himself for making the gains he was when Teddy's gallop took on a worse hitch, one that became a steady jerk, and finally a limp. He slowed. "You going to make it, Teddy?"

Give the old girl credit; she struggled and tried, as if she knew the nature of their purpose, sensed that a life depended on her. He eased up, but she didn't. She seemed to reach for a gallop, but slowed instead to a canter. She surged on with a strange new rhythm, three legs doing the bulk of the work of keeping them moving and maintaining a precarious balance that took extra strength.

Soon she was down to a trot, but one that gave her a beginning sheen of lather. For the first time, Justin feared he might well kill Teddy in his effort to save Francis. He didn't want that.

"Take it easy, girl. It's okay if we walk as long as we get there."
But she didn't listen, struggled on gallantly with all she had.
He worried for her sake. Worse, with her awkward gait, he began
to hear that stupid song Francis had made up playing again and
again in his head, though he was stuck on just one stanza.

Rode out of Salinas on a three-legged horse
Hard to say which of you's shot up the worse
A posse behind and Comanches ahead
A flat piece of rock may well be your last bed.

The darned thing went around and around in his head,
wouldn't stop. The jostling steps his poor horse was making
finally pulled him out of that. He patted her rump, wanted her
to know she was doing as good a job as she could.

He felt a lump in his throat. "Please don't do yourself in,
Teddy." In a moment he was going to have to rein her in to save
her life. Then, in the distance he saw the tail end of the column
of Rangers. "Hey!" he yelled.

Coming at an angle he made up the difference in distance in
spite of Teddy's slower pace.

"Hey!"

One of them heard him, turned, must have shouted up the
column, which slowed and came to stop. The men at the rear of
the column had bandannas pulled up over their faces so they
looked like so many bank robbers. Pale white dust covered their
shirts, hats, and what parts of their faces that showed.

"We made it, Teddy. We made it." He could have cried, maybe
already was crying. Hard to tell with the wind in his face. She
was a brave old gal, and had done all she could.

He pulled hard and slowed to a halt just as she got to the
men. She stood quivering, one leg lifted off the ground, and
blowing as hard as any horse Justin had ever seen getting its
breath back. "Please don't die on me now, Teddy."

But she didn't look ready to do that. Her big eye fixed on Justin as she turned her head to look back to him as if to say, "We did it. I knew we could all along."

The back end group of Rangers broke their ranks, which must have ticked off Lieutenant Cawley to no end, and at the head of them, pulling down the mask from his face and rushing to Justin was Jobe Jenkins, who Justin thought of as an old friend by now.

They crowded around. Jobe hopped down off his horse, gave Justin a hand dismounting.

"Zed, do you have that liniment?"

One of the other Rangers who had helped Justin, Francis, and Lucas to town dug in a saddlebag and tossed a brown bottle to Jobe, who began rubbing the liquid onto Teddy's leg.

"Where are you coming from that you'd ride a horse half to death like that?"

"Francis is shot. I need you to get him to where he can be helped."

"Cawley will never go for that." The Ranger who said it rode closer and climbed down from his saddle.

"This is Sergeant Stubbs, as you may recall," Jobe said.

Justin remembered, though he knew Jobe better.

"How did Francis get shot?" Jobe asked.

Justin was still breathing deeply from his ride. He took another deep breath, said, "Bentley's and Kenedy's men are going at it over in a valley yonder. Too far to hear the shots from here. There might be Indians too."

Lieutenant Cawley came riding back along the column and then up to them, his hair waving back behind him. He scowled.

"We need to take care in how we pitch this, Jenkins," Stubbs said, his voice getting lower. "Cawley's all right when he gets a chance to go rough and ready, but he's young and still has a lot of cavalry stuck in him."

"You'd better give us all you've got," Jobe said to Justin. "I have a notion you haven't told us everything, and we need some ammo here. We're going to need the works."

He and Stubbs and Jobe put their heads close together. He would have liked to hold back about Aunt Sara's gold. But Francis's life might well be in the balance. He told Jobe everything and finished just as Cawley got all the way to them.

"Now, what's going on that has slowed us like this?"

"You'd better tell him," Stubbs said to Justin.

Justin repeated for the lieutenant's benefit, "Bentley's and Kenedy's men are going at it over in a valley yonder. Too far to hear the shots from here. There might be Indians too."

"You hear that, Lieutenant?" Stubbs said. "You've got a right proper stack of chips here: a first-class feud, over murders and rustling, with Injuns thrown in for a bargain."

He was selling it strong, but Justin didn't mind. "Don't forget. We need to rescue Francis, too. He's been shot," he added.

"You hear that?" Stubbs let a lot of enthusiasm ripple through the words. "A rescue, too, as icing on the cake. This one's got stars and spangles on it."

"We have our orders. Get our butts down to the border." Cawley looked at the string of his men, still in the columns waiting for his orders. He looked a little torn, but had made up his mind.

Jobe gave a quick nod to Justin, who said, "I guess we won't be able to recover that gold, then."

"Gold?" Cawley's head snapped back to him. "What gold?"

"My uncle Roger was a Union quartermaster. When they pulled out for the war, he hid the payroll, all gold coin. He left my father and then me a map. The Bentley bunch came to Aunt Sara's house and stole that money. They have the gold with them right now."

"Is that what they're fighting over?" Cawley asked.

"No. I get the notion Kenedy doesn't even know about the gold," Jobe said. "They're going at it because they each think the other bunch was rustling, and they're both right."

Justin could see in Cawley's thoughtful frown that mere rustlers and a right proper feud didn't weigh all that much to him. But rescuing lost federal money might well teeter the scales in his decision.

"And there's the gold," Jobe reminded him.

"Recovering federal gold is just the sort of thing that shows bright when someone's being considered for a captaincy," Stubbs said.

Lieutenant Cawley surprised Justin and shared a smile for the first time. "Well, I suppose those desperadoes can wait a day. Are we Rangers or are we not?"

"Rangers!" the men shouted.

"Stubbs, assign someone to watch this hurt horse and the burros. The rest of us are off at a pace to mix it up."

Sergeant Stubbs pointed to Zed. For a second Zed looked disappointed, then shrugged and took Teddy's reins and reached for the liniment bottle Jobe held. "Come on, old girl. By the time they come back we'll have you square-dancing."

"Better loan me your horse, Zed," Jobe said. "Justin can ride it there, and climb on back of me for the way back. You recall what a bruiser that Francis is."

Justin mounted Zed's horse and moved up close to Jobe.

"Break formation, men!" Cawley shouted. "We're going to be riding hard and fast here."

He spun and was off with such a jump on the others, they had their hands full getting their horses to catch up with him. They rode as a loose happy pack this time. Rangers off to do some Rangering.

Chapter Twenty-Five

So this is what it was like to be riding with a group of as ready and seasoned a bunch of men as he'd ever seen. Justin felt a pride he couldn't believe, and if someone had handed him a paper right then to sign on as a Ranger, he'd have signed it. Not likely to happen, but darned nice to think about.

The miles peeled by, and they made short work of the distance that had taken Teddy quite a spell to cover.

Justin had been so concerned about her making it at all that he hadn't paid as much attention as usual to landmarks. But all he had to do was point these Rangers in the right general direction, and they picked up the rest from the unusual limping trail Teddy had left for them.

Soon he could make out the mesa ahead, this side of it, and it grew larger as they neared it. The Rangers rode up to it and followed its lower edge toward the other side.

Justin could hear shots still being fired as the Rangers pounded around the base of the mesa. He pulled close to Jobe, yelled, "Francis is over this way."

Jobe signaled to Bo, and the three of them peeled off while the others were already rounding the corner of the mesa and heading into the valley. At first the sounds of shooting picked up, then settled into a sporadic exchange that hinted the Rangers had hit the ground and were moving forward in a systematic sweep.

Whatever mess was going on in there, the survivors shouldn't make matters worse by shooting at Rangers. But maybe no one was handy to tell them that.

Justin led the way to where he'd left Francis. He half hoped to see him scurrying out to greet them. But Jobe and Bo together had to ease into the scrub and help pull Francis to his feet.

"Stiffened up lying there that long. Thought I was half a corpse. Man alive, I was cheered, though, by hearing shod horses coming my way."

"You saw Indians?" Jobe stepped closer.

"Yep, and they had leather stockings on the hooves of their horses and were sweeping brush behind as they went. I doubt you'll find a single print."

Jobe spun to Bo. "There. You see? That's how they did it at the Kenedy spread."

Bo nodded. He was looking around. But if he saw any Indian sign, he didn't say.

Jobe and Bo got Francis's crusty shirt off and Jobe got out a patching plaster for each side of the wound. "This should do till we get you to a doc." He rubbed the outer edges of the wound clean, didn't try to mess with the scab that was forming. The flesh around the wound had a purple tinge by now and had swollen. "You should be fine once we get you to town. Bo and I both been shot worse'n this."

"You might go up to the mesa top and see if Bentley's son Esau is still there. I popped him a pretty good lick, but he was still breathing when we left him."

Bo took his long gun and resting sticks and started up the slope. "Might be able to lay down some cover fire while I'm up there."

But they couldn't hear any more shooting from where they were.

Jobe got the patching plasters into place on Francis, then he and Justin helped wrestle the shirt back on.

Francis scowled, still probably feeling a pretty good throb from his wound.

Jobe took in the way the shirt barely covered Francis and the big man's expression. "My, if you don't look like a bear that's just crawled out of a cave after a bad hibernation."

Francis managed half a grin at that, then winced.

They were helping Francis get up into the saddle of Zed's horse as Bo came back down the slope at a pretty good pace and joined them.

"Find him?" Jobe said.

"What's left of him. Someone's slit his throat."

"Wasn't us. Neither Justin nor I even have a belt knife. Do you think some Comanche did it?"

"That's exactly what I think," Bo said, "even though his scalp hasn't gone missing too. I think someone's playing a game here."

"Bent Feather," Jobe said.

Bo nodded.

Justin could hear the sounds of sporadic shooting, sometimes lifting into flurries, then dying back to exchanged shots. The noise grew louder as they rounded the bottom of the mesa and headed toward the heart of the melee.

By the time they got around to the other side of the mesa, Justin peered out from behind Jobe and saw that the fighting had progressed pretty much the way he'd figured. Coming up on them from behind, the Rangers had battled their way through the Kenedy bunch, and those who didn't lie about on the ground and weren't ever going to rise again were sitting in irons in a row out of the way of the shooting. Justin didn't see Kenedy himself among them. Perhaps if he'd fallen early, the others would have given up and left, since they didn't know about the gold. Just when Justin was about to give up looking for him, a figure rose up from near the end of the rock-pile defense behind which all of the Bentley bunch still alive were huddled and firing out at the Rangers now. The figure was Kenedy.

Even from here, and jostling along on the back end of Old Top, Justin saw another figure rise up from behind the rock cover. Old Captain Bentley himself. Ignoring the incoming fire from the Rangers, he stood half a dozen feet from Kenedy. The two of them had to be looking right into each other's eyes. They fired shot after shot until they'd emptied their pistols. They stood there a moment, quivering in place, then both crumpled to the ground at once. If Justin had ever in his life seen anything more stupid, he didn't know what it was.

Bentley falling like that took the last of the steam out of his men. The Kenedy side had already called it quits, except the old man himself, and it didn't look like he'd rise again.

Bo was among those who went in to clear out the area behind the rock cover. He looked their way and shook his head. That was the end of Bentley and Kenedy, and a sure-enough end to anything resembling a feud.

Stubbs and the other Rangers were mostly on a cleanup detail, gathering up what horses they could, and getting the bodies together for an accounting. Only five of the Kenedy bunch had survived. Less than that, only three, climbed out from where the Bentley bunch had taken cover. One more had to be carried, but he didn't last long enough for them to get him to where the other survivors were trying on their irons. Justin looked hard, but didn't see Gabe Bentley among the prisoners or among the bodies being stretched out in rows.

Some of the Rangers were tending to the wounds of their own men. All of the Rangers were still alive, though a couple had lost their horses. There were plenty of other horses, still with saddles on, to choose from. Rangers were gathering them into a string. A couple of the prisoners groaned, but the Rangers went on tending their own first—seemed many had the makings of rough first aid in their saddlebags, since getting shot at a lot seemed to be their fare.

"Damnedest thing," Cawley said as Jobe rode up with Justin behind him.

"Let me guess. Some men on the fringes of Kenedy's bunch had their throats cut," Jobe said.

"How the devil did you know that?" Cawley tilted his head at him.

"We've parsed out that Bent Feather was behind some of this. He's probably the one killed those folks at Kenedy's ranch house. Made it look like Bentley's bunch did it. All they had to do was leave a single Bentley branding iron behind, and the whole Kenedy bunch was off on the warpath."

"Really? You're trying to convince me that some blasted redskin's clever enough to put all that in motion? That this Bent Feather's clever enough to have played these two bunches against each other?"

"I think he's every bit that clever and more," Jobe said.

"Really?"

"Well, those Kenedy men didn't cut their own throats. And Bentley's men couldn't do that from where they were pinned down. I reckon Bent Feather's bunch thinned out a few of the Kenedys so the fight was more even. I suppose he hoped both sides would wipe out each other."

"If that's the case, he wasn't far wrong. Bentley is dead. Kenedy's a goner as well. Still, it's hard to believe that part about the redskins."

"Bentley's other son is dead up on top of that mesa. Slit throat too, and I'm willing to bet he didn't cut himself while shaving."

Cawley lifted the front of his hat brim up an inch with a finger. "Well, I'm blamed if I understand it, or more than half believe it. Why a Comanche clever as that would make old

Buffalo Hump himself proud."

"It's the only way it all parses out, Lieutenant."

"Why haven't you rounded the rascal up before now, then?"

Stubbs shook his head. "There, sir, I believe you're asking for something even beyond the power of Rangers. That Injun is one ghost if I ever saw one. But if you want, we can give it all we have. Should we go after him?"

"Only if you ride on unicorns to do so. Now let's have a look at this gold."

The lieutenant kneeled down by the saddlebags Bo had fetched from the Bentleys' horses. He took the bags out and laid them all in a row. Jobe and Stubbs had moved close to watch, and they led the horse carrying Francis. He sat upright, hanging onto the saddle horn to stay in the saddle. Justin watched him sway and hoped he could last until they got him to a doctor.

Cawley looked up at Justin and Francis. "Is this all the gold these men took from the lady's house?"

"Looks to be all there," Francis said.

Justin nodded. He didn't mention the handful of coins Bentley had given Lucas before sending him off to what he probably thought was his death. It didn't seem the sort of detail to bring up just now.

"Are you going to give that back to Sara Bolger?" Francis asked. "It's hers by rights. Those Bentleys stole it from the lady, who was only going to use it to pay her taxes. They robbed her. It's as plain and simple as that. We were there when it happened."

"It's true," Justin said, then under his breath, "sort of."

"You'll have to do better than that, fellows. I didn't just roll off the turnip wagon. I know what a government payroll looks like, and this one's been listed missing from these parts since the Union closed down the fort for the big misunderstanding

between the states. That money belongs to the federal government, such as it is."

"Couldn't we have just enough of it to cover Sara Bolger's
taxes, sir?" Francis said.

"It's a bold enough try. But no." Cawley looked about. "Now,
do we have enough to charge the Kenedy survivors with rustling?"

"Seems to me they were stealing each other's cattle back and
forth," Stubbs chimed in. "You'd have to charge the Bentleys as
well, and the ones responsible are dead, as dead as Kenedy."

"Not all the Bentleys are dead," Jobe spoke up. "At least I
don't think so. I haven't seen Gabe's body, and he isn't one of
those in irons. Maybe he sneaked off the way Esau was trying to
do."

"I doubt we'd have enough to charge him for anything, and
we have the gold." Cawley gave the sacks a touch with the toe
of his boot. "May have to let that go."

"What about the stage robbery? I think the Bentley boys are
good for that." Stubbs looked at Jobe Jenkins as he said it. "And
maybe the liveryman Sid as well. We can squeeze him, and I
expect he'll sing like a canary once we search the Bentley house
and find that money."

"The boys would steal the payroll their father was having
sent to town?" Cawley said.

"Man was tight, wouldn't give the boys any money for liquor
or women, and they both had hobbies in those areas," Stubbs
said. "Jenkins there did most of the fancy footwork on this."

"We find that stage money at the house after the captain has
already made a claim with the stage company for it, and we've
got a right proper bow tied on all this after all. Now let's gather
up this gold and the prisoners and head to town."

"You going to be okay?" Justin called over to Francis.

His eyes were bloodshot and pink with the pain of jostling

along in the saddle. He spoke through clenched teeth. "What say we just ride."

CHAPTER TWENTY-SIX

Lucas reined in his horse and eased her down the grassy slope to the shore of the creek she'd smelled from a few miles back. She was turning out to be a right clever mare. Vin's gelding caught up and carried him down to the rill of water. Soon the two horses were drinking while Lucas dismounted and sat on a wide log of what looked to be a dead cypress. Vin climbed down and joined him. For a while the two sat in silence. Lucas savored the bubbling sound of water as it passed, the sight of the horses getting their fill. They'd have plenty more miles in them after this. He'd fill his canteen in a minute, upstream, but for now he wanted to sit a spell.

"I've got a iron skillet and some beans," Vin said.

"I don't fancy staying out here too long." Lucas looked around. "That dern Bent Feather may be any old where."

"We going to ride off together?"

"Doubt it. We most always rub each other the wrong way 'fore long. I believe I'll amble over to Abilene."

"Laredo's sounding good to me. Man could make some money down there."

"Just don't let some young buck come gunning for the Vinegar Kid down there."

"You're getting a name yourself. That Kenedy fellow knew to send for you."

"He was willing to spend me quick enough, let you gun me down if it gave him time and a distraction enough to get to cover. Only way I make sense of it."

"None of them's figured out yet that you were always the fast one."

"Wouldn't have done me much good if I'd ended my days out there staked in the sun by those dern Injuns."

"Did you make anything out of this mess?"

"Got a handful of coin from Bentley. It was like giving a quart of his blood, it pained him so to let go of it. You want some of that?"

"No. I got Kenedy to cough up early. He didn't like it. But what the hell? These guys didn't get rich by giving anything away." Vin thought a moment. "You know, we could ride over to the Bentley ranch and poke around while they're occupied. Probably a fair bit of money lying about."

"I don't see us doing that. We're a lot of things, but being thieves isn't one of them." Lucas settled one hand on the pocket that held the gold. He'd earned that.

"You know, Mom always said that having two boys was too many. She considered drowning one of us."

"Should have been you."

The horses had finished drinking and were tucking into the grass that formed a rich carpet just above the rocky shoal.

Lucas rose and got his canteen. He took a few steps up the creek and let it fill, took a sip or two, and topped it off again. Vin did the same.

They ambled back to the horses, and Lucas swung up into his saddle.

Vin did the same, then tipped his hat to Lucas. "See you around."

"Not if I see you first."

They rode off in different directions.

★　★　★　★　★

Bent Feather rode with his three remaining Comanche warriors. Not much of a war party now that the two Kiowa had gone back to the reservation to melt back in with their tribe. That was no longer an option for Bent Feather, for a number of reasons. Chief among them was that he was known now, and folks were hunting for him. Didn't bother him. But it worried him about a young buck like Sleeping Bear. Eager and almost clever enough to get by, though it took a lot more cleverness these days than it ever used to.

In the distance he could see the Bentley ranch house. He rode a bit farther until he could no longer see it, or be seen from it. Those men were away, but it was best to be cautious. He was always cautious.

When they were far enough from the buildings, Sleeping Bear tugged the bow from over his shoulder and pointed to a calf just straying from its mother who was poking into the lusher green of an arroyo to eat.

Bent Feather nodded, and the boy rode off as if he were back in the happy days of heading into a buffalo herd. He carried a long gun and could use it, but Bent Feather was glad he still favored the old and quieter ways to hunt. That could always be useful.

No, it no longer felt like the buffalo days. Those days were all behind them. He should ride off up into the Llano Estacado. But who would that leave to pester the whites, remind them of whose land they had taken?

Sleeping Bear gave a shout. Jumped off his horse at the fallen calf and began to cut the parts they could use now and dry for later. Best to dry a lot of it, all they could. They might have to ride.

As evening settled, they kept a low fire going far out of sight from the ranch house. A low creek that had dried to a mere ripple ran beside their camp.

The boy looked up at Bent Feather, the flicker of light from the fire showing as eager sparks in his eyes. He still spoke Comanche, though he could sign if the need ever arose to speak with the white devils. "I'd like to be called Roadrunner."

Bent Feather nodded.

"We'll see," he told him.

CHAPTER TWENTY-SEVEN

All the way back on the ride to where they'd left Zed with the burros and Teddy, Justin kept a close eye on Francis, who had started out sitting up in the saddle but had gradually slumped. He'd lost more than a chunk of his shirt. He'd lost a fair bit of blood, and now would be a good time to be stretched out in a bed instead of jostling along on horseback.

Jobe rode close to one side of him, with Justin clinging on behind, and Bo rode the other side, in case Francis showed signs of falling out of the saddle. Though, big as he was, Justin wasn't sure how they planned to catch him.

He was a sight. No more burgundy velvet-covered fop with silk handkerchief. Rather now, belly hanging out a bit from a shirt that had long ago quit being white, stubble on his chin heading toward becoming a beard, he looked more like a wounded bear being brought home to its zoo. Yet Justin now liked and cared for the big lump of a man more than he ever had before.

Several times Francis swayed in the saddle, looked half ready to tumble, then he'd shake himself and sit up straighter. There appeared to be tougher stuff in him than just being a slinger of words.

Cawley had loosened the order of their return, so they rode in one big group, he and his men guarding a line of prisoners strung along in a roped line on horses that had survived the melee. A few of the saddled horses that had survived the shooting followed in a remuda string after the prisoners. The lieutenant guarded the gold himself, with a couple of his men riding close. The feathers in his hat bobbed along in the ride, but this was going to be an even bigger feather in his cap when he turned in the recovered federal money.

Justin sighed. That would have gone a long ways toward saving Aunt Sara's farm. For him, the landscape rolled by. Not needing to pay close attention to the limping Teddy to see if she could make it, or even guide a horse along at all, Justin took in the scenery of the area he was coming to feel was his new home. Wide stretches of grass, stone jutting up here and there in almost any place he looked, stands of taller trees near any sign of water, and cactus and low brush in clumps, almost all of the growth bearing some sort of sticker or other. Forbidding as it was, he was coming to love the land too, and hate it. But mostly love it. He took a deep dusty breath of air.

They paused once at a stream, and once more so the men could pour water from their canteens into cupped hands to let their horses wet their whistles.

Jobe stood by his horse Old Top, looking ready to climb back on. Justin started that way. As he got near, Jobe twitched his head for Justin to come closer.

"What?" Justin said.

"There were a couple of other bodies missing in that count back there." Jobe stared hard into Justin's eyes. "You happen to know anything about that?"

"Well, there was Lucas Brent and that preacher."

"Yeah, go on."

"Seems they had to square off against each other. You know, the two fastest guns, or something like that, the way Francis explained it."

"And?"

"They buffaloed everyone by just riding off."

"No one tried to stop them?"

"Would you?"

"I guess not."

"In all the excitement of getting help for Francis, it slipped my mind. And to tell you the truth, it had me more than a mite confused. Should I have told Sergeant Stubbs and Lieutenant Cawley about it?"

"It would probably just confuse them too. It has me. Now, what say we ride?" He climbed up in the saddle and reached down for Justin's arm.

By the time they all arrived at a spot where Zed sat with the two burros and Teddy under the sprawling dark shade of a live oak, Francis looked pretty done in, but refused to get off the saddle. "I'll never to be able to get myself back on," he muttered.

"We could build him a travois," Jobe suggested, "but like as not it'd jostle him worse than just staying on the back of that horse, and town's not too far away from here."

Justin nodded. He went over to Teddy.

Zed had a currycomb out and was brushing her. Her coat shined, and she gave a low whinny of recognition as Justin came close and rubbed her forehead down to her muzzle. Zed had not only rubbed in liniment, but had taken a strip of the first-aid gauze and tape and put it around her leg to give her some support.

"How's she doing?"

"She's gonna be fine," Zed said. "I wouldn't ride her just yet. But a few good weeks of pasture time and she should last you for years to come. She is right plumb full of the best kind of good grit."

Zed looked through and picked out a horse from those that no longer had riders, since Francis was still glued to the saddle of his horse. Justin didn't mind riding the rest of the way back behind Jobe, so he climbed back up to his seat there.

The next stretch of riding seemed to whir by for Justin, and probably Francis as well, since he had all he could do to stay in the saddle. Several times they thought he'd topple off. But at last Justin looked up and saw they were coming into the edge of town. Jobe peeled off from the others, and he led Francis on Zed's horse up to a small white house standing alone. A hand-painted sign out front said: "Dr. F. W. Willis."

Justin and Jobe dismounted. Jobe went to the front door and pounded on it. "Is Doc Willis in?"

"Of course I'm in. Where the devil would I go? No reason to pound the door like it's the collapse of civilization as we know it. Door's open. What d'you want?"

"We've got a shot man here."

"We'll that's a new one for me."

"Really?"

"Of course not. Either bring him in or bury him out there. I don't care which."

Jobe glanced to Justin. They exchanged a shrug.

Doc Willis turned out to be far less crabby once they'd carefully gotten a wobbly Francis off the horse and down the small walkway to the door. Inside, Doc Willis looked up from spreading a sheet across a wooden table in the middle of the room. He grinned at them. White hair tugged to the back of his head and tied in a knot. Rectangular wire-rim glasses were propped on his nose. He looked like a doctor, and that reassured Justin.

"Mostly get croup and cholera, except for gunshots. I get a whole lot of gunshots."

"There'll be a couple of Rangers and a few prisoners you may get to tend to next. But this one's in a needy way." Jobe helped Justin and the doctor ease Francis onto the tabletop.

Francis closed his eyes, looked exhausted enough to welcome a nap, or at least lying down and being off the back of a horse.

Doc Willis cut away the shirt and whistled low. "Someone did a pretty good job on you, fella. Probably saved your life."

Francis's eyes fluttered open. He looked toward Jobe and Justin.

"We won't linger," Jobe said. "We have some chores, and looking for the whereabouts of Gabe Bentley is one of them."

"Let me . . . let me talk to the boy a minute," Francis managed. He lifted a hand, then let it plop back to the table.

Doc Willis was busy putting some scalpels, tools, and bandage material on the small table next to where he planned to work on Francis.

"I want you to dig in my pockets, Justin, and fetch out that fancy lady's gun and the extra bullets." The gun they'd taken from Esau had fallen out of Francis' belt somewhere in the course of getting him here.

"Why?"

"Well, for one thing, because I sure as Hades don't need them just now, and you might."

"Really?"

"If Gabe and his brother were involved in that stage robbery like Jobe there thinks, then you have the rare opportunity a man gets to face the person who killed your father."

"Revenge? I hadn't thought about that."

"Well, do so. How do you feel?"

"I said at the time, that I wished the person dead. I guess I still do. But I've never killed anyone before."

"And you're not going to get the chance now if I have anything to say about it," Jobe said.

"Let him have the gun for his own protection, then. Such as it is."

"Can't hurt, I reckon."

Jobe fetched the small gun and extra bullets out of Francis's pockets. The derringer seemed mighty small, but the bullets inside it were deadly enough. He put them in his own pockets.

"At least be my eyes and ears. I wish I could go with you. This is the really good and juicy stuff."

"Like as not the lieutenant may not even want Jobe to go after Gabe," Justin said. "He seemed pretty content with the coup of getting the gold recovered."

"Shame about that." Francis's voice was beginning to sound weaker and more frail. "You let Sara know we did the best we could about that." He lifted his head, tried to rise by pushing up with one elbow, but Doc Willis was able to press him back down to the table with one hand.

Francis turned his head sideways to look at Justin. "You can trust Jobe, son. I don't know enough about that lieutenant yet. Shouldn't go on my first impression."

"This Cawley is no fool," Jobe said. "Don't you think that of the man. He might seem as though he likes starch in his linen, but you don't make Ranger lieutenant by not knowing what you're up to, and with who you're dealing. He's just careful, and maybe a little proper. There's nothing wrong with that out here."

Justin didn't know why Jobe had spoken up on behalf of his lieutenant, but for reasons he didn't fully understand, he was glad Jobe had.

"Now, if you fellas would mosey out of here, I've got work to do here and more waiting for me later," Doc Willis said. His blue eyes sparkled behind his glasses. A man who knew what he was doing and liked his work.

Outside they got on the two horses and rode to the sheriff's office, where several of the horses had been tied. Others were tied over by the general store, where some of the Rangers must be rounding up the supplies for the long ride down to the border. None of the Ranger horses were tied at the saloon, and that said something about Cawley's sense of order.

Justin tried to take in other details of the town, savor being back in so-called civilization after quite a hairy adventure out in the wilds. But his mind stayed fixed on one thing. Gabe Bentley. When his father lay there, yes, he had felt a rage and might have wanted revenge. But could Justin do it? Given the chance, did he have what it took? It seemed expected of him, and he had to pause and explore his innermost feelings. Could he hate enough, did he hate enough, for that? Was it, in fact, the right and only thing to do?

They tied their horses to the crowded rail outside the sheriff's office. At the door, Justin hesitated, looked out and around at the town. Not much to see. One or two horsemen riding, a woman loading goods from the general store into a buggy, and small dust devils rising, swirling, in the middle of the wide dirt street that passed through the town. Streets wide so cattle could be driven through, saloon and fancy-lady house to entertain the cowhands when they had any pay and time to spend. A jail for when they played too hard. It was a cattle town, and it had just lost two of its biggest cattlemen. Jobe went inside and Justin followed.

Lieutenant Cawley sat behind the desk, a stack of wanted posters in front of him. He leafed through them, occasionally glancing back at the two small cells, where the prisoners had been crowded.

"Where's the sheriff?" Jobe glanced around.

"Long gone. I found just his badge lying on the desk when I came in. Word travels fast, and with Bentley no longer around, I guess he decided his pastures were greener elsewhere. Another smart man."

"Smart enough," Jobe agreed.

Stubbs sat in a straight-backed chair over by the cell doors. He nodded to Jobe, then sat and waited, as patient as Rome waiting on Hannibal to make it over the Alps with his elephants.

A groan came from one of the wounded men in the cells.

"Doc Willis can tend to any wounds, as soon as he finishes with Francis and then the Rangers." Jobe glanced toward the cells. "Any of these men worth anything?"

"Three of them so far, as well as a couple of the dead we left back there. I've dispatched men with a wagon to bring the bodies in before the coyotes can get at them. I'm just glad no Rangers were worse than wounded."

Stubbs rose. "Why don't I go round up our wounded and get them over to the doctor so he can get busy on them?"

Cawley nodded. "Good idea, Sergeant."

When Stubbs had gone out the door, Jobe asked Cawley, "You mind if I take a quick peek through those wanted posters?"

Cawley frowned. "No, I guess not. Anything particular on your mind?"

"Not yet." Jobe went through them quickly, only once pausing to look more closely at a particular poster. Shook his head, and slid the stack back to Cawley. "Thank you, sir."

"Find what you were looking for?"

"Nope."

The lieutenant looked up at Jobe, as if he'd been indulgent and too patient so far. "Now, let's talk about the stage robbers. You claim the Bentley boys were in on it. Why?"

"A line of tracks of three horses led back to this town from the stage robbery, a distinctive set of hoofprints since one of the horses was carrying a bent nail in one shoe. The liveryman, Sid, denied reshoeing a horse, but I think he lied. I looked at Bentley's bunch of horses, and the horse with the repaired shoe belonged to Esau."

"Who's dead."

"Right. But Gabe was nowhere in that group after the scrap. He's still alive and is around, somewhere. As is the money from

187

the stage robbery."

Cawley looked down at the bags of gold coin piled onto the desk. "I've already wired the captain about this. He wired back that a troop of cavalry is on its way to pick it up. He was mighty pleased."

"He'd be more pleased if the stage robbery was handed to him with a bow as well." Jobe had shifted from parade rest to nearly attention, Justin noticed. He must want something.

"We can't just go out to the Bentley place and nose around for Gabe or that money," Cawley said. "You do know about the Fourth Amendment. Normally I'd get the sheriff's help rounding up a warrant from a judge, but since that doesn't seem likely . . ."

"There might be another way," Jobe interrupted.

"Talk to me. I'm listening."

"The livery. There were three of them in on the stage robbery. The Bentleys owned the livery. That Sid fellow might have been the third rider with the two Bentley boys."

"Who you claim robbed the stage because their tightfisted father wouldn't share any of his with them?"

"It's the way I see it, sir."

Well, there you have it, Justin thought. Whenever Jobe trucked out a *sir*, he was definitely after something.

"Let me get a detail to watch this money and the prisoners," Cawley said, "and then we'll go have us a look."

With three men in place guarding the sheriff's office, Lieutenant Cawley, Jobe and Justin left their horses behind and walked down the street to the livery. A couple of sets of wrist irons clattered lightly from where they hung from the lieutenant's belt. Cawley glanced toward Justin, who tagged along, but didn't say anything until they got to the livery.

They didn't see Sid out front.

"Let's give him a surprise treat and come around from the other side," Cawley said.

Jobe nodded.

Cawley turned to Justin. "You stay here. Don't take a step inside. Okay?"

Justin nodded, but as they slipped around the side of the building, his hand slid into his pocket and he held the derringer. Could he do it? Well, we'll see, he thought. If what Jobe had said was true, Sid had been one of those who had robbed the stage, wrecked it, killed his father in the process, and left them all for dead.

Wind whipped a light spray of dust and sandy grit against the front of the livery, making a raspy sound. A horse whinnied inside, another snorted. The smell of the livery wafted out to him, an aroma Justin didn't find all that offensive now. Horses were fine animals. He'd seen Teddy among the other horse tied outside the general store, but hadn't had the chance to go see how she was doing.

The seconds ticked by as the Rangers' getting in from the back way seemed to be taking a long time.

"Hey. Hold still there!" He heard feet pounding the hard dirt ground. Sid came running, got half out the front door before he was yanked back inside. Justin could see Jobe right behind the man, pulling at him. He heard the two of them hit the ground, and what sounded like them wrestling in there.

A creak above Justin's head gave away the upper-floor door swinging open. There, in the open loading door to the hayloft crouched Gabe Bentley, his gun drawn in one hand. He jumped for the ground, landed with bent knees, rolled, and then stood upright, looking right at Justin.

Justin's hand snapped up. He pointed the derringer right at Gabe, who laughed.

"You've got to be kidding me." Same thing his brother had said.

He swung the gun in his hand up to point at Justin.

Justin lowered the barrel of the derringer and squeezed the trigger.

Bam! Little gun, big-assed bullet. The gun bucked in his hand like a rabid animal.

The bullet slammed into the outside of Gabe's thigh, spun him around. He dropped his gun and fell to the ground, but twisted to stare at Justin. "A kid. I've been shot by a kid!"

Cawley came tearing out the front door of the livery, took in everything at a glance. He kicked away the fallen six-shooter and crouched down to flip Gabe over and lock his wrists together behind him.

"Got this one," Cawley yelled. "How're you coming along in there with Sid?"

"Just fine. He's decided to pass out on me."

Cawley didn't ask. Instead, he called out, "Let's get him locked up and this other one to the doc. We've got one more for him to work on, but see that he doesn't get in line before all the Rangers have been tended to."

"A kid. I've been shot by a blasted kid," Gabe was still muttering while Cawley got him turned upright and scooched back until his back was against the livery's wall.

"Better fetch a wagon."

"I'm going to get one hitched right away," Jobe called back from inside. "Hey, up here."

Justin saw him standing in the open second-floor loading door from which Gabe had jumped. He held up a couple of bags.

"Found the money too. It was up in the loft where Gabe was hiding. Still in the stage company bags. Stage shotgun's up here too. Has the company name stamped right on it. Can you believe that? Looks like you can check the stagecoach robbery off your list."

Cawley rose and looked at Justin.

The derringer felt warm in Justin's hand. He put it in his pocket and rubbed his hand on his pants. Firing it had sprayed some warm, stinging gunpowder onto his hand.

He stared down at Gabe. "He's lucky to be alive. I was aiming at his chest. Dern gun fires where it wants to, though."

CHAPTER TWENTY-EIGHT

Justin rode Teddy out along the side length of fence that went around the goat pen with Scamp hanging on close behind. Teddy's leg had mended quickly once she was able to stay off it for a few days and not have to struggle halfway across Texas—or so it seemed to Justin. Good feed and exercise had done her a lot of good, along with a lot of attention. Button went out to curry her whenever she could and rode Teddy herself when not doing chores in the garden. No one at the livery complained about her not being returned, what with Sid and Gabe being hauled away to wait on a stage-robbing trial and Captain Bentley no longer around. The livery was closed until someone figured out what to do with it.

Out on the lane, Justin made out a cloud of dust rising, more than what a single horse makes. As it grew close and he rode that way, he could make out the shape of a buggy. Then he could see Francis sitting on the buckboard's seat holding the reins.

The buggy pulled up in front of the fort at the same time Justin and Scamp got there on Teddy. They hopped off, looped Teddy's reins beside the well, and rushed toward the buggy.

Justin recognized the horse in the traces, Boots, who must have returned to the livery, not killed and eaten by those Comanche after all.

"Well, I see your horse recovered faster than I did," Francis called to them.

He wore a big buckskin shirt and appeared able to move his right arm well enough, though he seemed to take care while doing so.

Sara came out the front of the house as Francis was climbing down.

"I know. I know. I'm powerful slow in getting this to you. But here it is." He waved toward the back of the buggy where he had the mortar they needed to fix the hearth.

"We're just pleased to see you back and all in one piece. Justin told us you'd been shot."

"Yep. Doc Willis was kind enough to get me to a hotel room. As I was being helped out of his office, there was a line of Rangers and other men in irons all waiting to be patched. I felt quiet honored to be the first getting his attention."

"It's been a couple of weeks. Why don't you come inside? We can catch up. Nothing hot just yet until the fireplace is fixed back up."

"That's what I'm here for. To put that right, as I promised."

Justin and Scamp got busy taking the heavy bags inside. Each one carried two of them, and Justin wished for a second that Francis was well enough to help. But he'd loaded them into the buggy, hadn't he? Maybe this was another of his tests.

As soon as they were all inside, Sara said, "That Ranger, Jobe, stopped by. He was looking for you, but I explained you weren't back yet."

"He found me at the hotel. Had big news."

"What's that?" Sara pulled out a chair and may have expected to have to help Francis into it, but he just plopped down into place.

"Lieutenant Cawley resigned from the Rangers."

"Really? Why?"

"He admitted himself he was a little prim for the job. Recommended Stubbs to replace himself as lieutenant, and Jobe got promoted to sergeant. When they rode off, they promised to swing by and say howdy to you all when they get done down there on the border."

"Jobe left something for you here." Sara went over to the corner and came back carrying two bottles of red wine. "He said he found them at the Bentley place and they just fell into his saddlebags."

"I'll bet they did. But you can put them away, Sara. I'm giving that a rest for now. I have to keep alert, don't I, to direct the stone work Justin and Scamp will be doing?" He turned to them. "Now would someone dash out and fetch that little bundle I left on the seat?"

"I'll go." Button shot out the door at a run.

She was still the fastest of them. Justin had taken her on in a few dashes and she had been like a jackrabbit, left him behind every time. Button played when they had time to play, but had turned Justin down when he and Scamp had headed off to the creek for a swim to cool down. None of them had any duds but the clothes they wore, so they would have had to swim without clothes. Justin figured they all had a lot of time to get used to each other yet. It would come.

Button came back in at a run carrying the cloth bundle.

"Careful there," Francis said. He took the bundle from her and started to unwrap the red bandanna that contained another red-and-blue one inside.

"No more silk handkerchiefs, I see," Justin said.

Francis laughed. He untied the bandannas inside and took out two small crystal wine glasses. "There. I'm glad they made it. I sweated the whole way here about whether they could take the bumps and bounces in the road that were rattling me like a maraca."

"What am I to do with those?"

"I don't know. Entertain? If you decide just to give the wine to some church to use for communion, maybe you can throw in the glasses too. I just knew I owed you."

"Well, thank you, I think. Now there's something else I'd like to know."

"What's that?"

"How'd you come to buy a buckskin shirt?"

"Truth of it is it was the only shirt I could find in town that fit me. But won't I have fun, though, when I go back east wearing it. My publisher is going to say, 'Now, don't you just scream out-of-town.'"

"So you're heading back east, are you?"

"Of course. I hope you weren't thinking I was setting my cap for you. No offense, but I'd sooner wrestle a bobcat."

"Now, why would I find that offensive?" She grinned, though, in a way that said Francis couldn't have made her happier if he'd bought her flowers.

"Big as I am, you're way too much woman for me."

She just shared a wry twist of her mouth, still as pleased as she could be.

"Now you, Justin, and Scamp. Go fetch some water and something to mix up cement in. Daylight's a-burning. I'd like to get this hearth fixed so it can be drying and Sara can be back to making those wonderful soups of hers."

Scamp shot out the door. Before Justin followed, his eyes swept the lot of them. Sara, Missy, and finally Button. He caught Francis grinning at him. He spun and shot out the door. The West had certainly changed someone.

Jobe Jenkins sat at the tiny Los Robles cantina on the outskirts of Laredo, finally having his first break in the action and chance for a little entertainment. Bo and Zed sat at the table and the barmaid, Carmena, who kept flashing her smile and brown eyes at him, had just put a fresh glass of beer in front of each of them. Beads of sweat dotted the outsides of the glasses while a breeze, warm but at least moving, swept over them in the shade of the big oak tree under which they sat.

"Bo, you've got the eyes of a red-tailed hawk. Do you make out who's sitting inside there in that far back corner?"

"Hadn't noticed." Bo turned in his seat, squinted, then snapped back to stare at Jobe. "Why, that's Captain Marberry, of course. But . . ."

"And the fellow with him?"

"It's that preacher fella we run into not too awful long ago."

"That's what I thought."

Jobe gave it a spell. He and the others had been through a lot in a short time. He could stand to sit still. If he were prone to, he could have carved a few notches in his gun. They'd had quite a tussle with desperadoes so far, but being a Ranger, it was just regular days at work.

At first he was going to leave it alone. But when the preacher, the fellow he'd come to know later as Vin, the Vinegar Kid, rose, shook hands with Marberry and they'd slapped each other on the shoulder, Jobe rose. "Give me a minute here, guys, and order me another beer."

He slipped inside. It wasn't so dark as it had looked from outside. Jobe could see quite clearly now. Marberry saw him and gave him a short wave. Jobe went over, didn't try to sit down. A bottle and two glasses and Marberry's white hat sat on the table. Marberry was a great Ranger officer, but in off hours he often drifted off on his own, didn't encourage fraternizing closely with any of the men at those times. They respected that.

"What is it, Sergeant Jenkins?"

Jobe took that as a further discouragement from sitting down. He didn't intend to do so.

"Saw you inside, Cap, and thought I'd say howdy."

"Well, howdy, then."

"I was just wondering if you knew that man you were sitting with."

"Know him? Of course I do."

"It's just that I knew him as a preacher once. Then as the Vinegar Kid. I thought he was some kind of outlaw."

"A preacher?" Marberry laughed out loud. It took him almost a full minute to stop. "A preacher. Imagine that. I'll have to tell him. He'll get a belly laugh out of that."

"Well, who is he, if he isn't the Vinegar Kid?"

"Oh, he's the Vinegar Kid all right, these days, but he's no dern outlaw. Back a few years he was just Vin Thomas, a Ranger captain, just like me. Well, not just like. He was about ten times as handy. But he's no outlaw. Now he's got a brother, mind you, who could poison a well. Vin, though, is just a restless fella who likes to amble around to where things are stirring. Why, did you come to know him?"

"No. Not very well, sir. Not very well at all."

The stagecoach rolled in from one end of the town of Bentley and came to a stop in front of the hotel. A driver and guard riding shotgun rode up top behind the horses. Justin, Aunt Sara, who was holding Missy's hand, Button, and Scamp stood beside Francis, who still wore his buckskin shirt, proudly, it seemed to Justin.

"Hey." Sheriff Cawley came half jogging up the street. "Don't you run off without me getting in a good-bye to you."

The sheriff sure looked different to Justin, not so rigid or stuffy as he had when he was a Ranger. Was that even a wrinkle in his shirt collar? No, just the light shining on it funny. Some things don't change that fast or much.

Cawley came to a stop and held out a hand. Francis shook it. His strength was back enough to just about jostle Cawley out of his boots. The sheriff wore a star on his shirt and looked happier than Justin thought he'd ever seen him. "Town has sure enough changed since you first saw it, with the Bentleys and Kenedy gone."

Francis nodded. He seemed a better listener now, less the booming big voice.

"I imagine you rounded up plenty of new fodder for those yarns of yours."

Francis grinned. "Enough I probably won't have to come out this way again for a long, long time. Though who knows, I might grow restless and miss this darned place." His eyes locked briefly with Sara's, moved on quickly to Justin. "You sure you want to stay and work on the farm, see what happens, grow a bit?"

Justin nodded. "Are you sure you want to ride a stage going back after what happened last time?"

"I might as well enjoy. The railroads coming along like they are will soon enough change all this. But that's okay, because change always gives me what I need for writing."

Then Francis bent down, still a little stiffly, and hugged the kids one by one, even Justin, and spent a little longer hugging Sara.

He had no luggage, so he climbed up into the stage and closed the door. He looked out the window and waved as the driver cracked the whip and the team took off. They all waved back as the stage rolled down the street and was soon out of sight.

Justin sighed. "I'm sorry, Aunt Sara, but we weren't able to get the gold back for you."

"That's all right. We'll get by somehow."

"A person can only do as much as he can do."

"Oh." Cawley turned to Sara. "Didn't he tell you?"

"Tell me what?"

"He got his publisher to agree to pay your taxes for you. Said it was the least he could do. They already wired the money."

Sara's eyes opened wide. She took half a step back.

"What's more, he's arranged to pay the taxes for the next five years, so you can have time to get back on your feet. Now all you have to do is keep selling produce and what you can make from the goats."

"Oh, my stars."

She looked down the street where the dust was settling.

"That's not all," Cawley said. "Seems Randall Morton over at the general store is itching to pay you for the past produce he's bought from you, and he wants to order more. I don't know what happened. Maybe it's Bentley being gone. But I have a sneaking feeling that big fella who just left had a chat with Randall. Leastwise, Randall wouldn't look me in the eye when I asked about it."

Cawley was still chuckling as he walked back up the street toward his office. A couple of people waved him a howdy as he went by. He was already fitting in just fine.

Justin stared off in the direction the stage had rolled away. "Well, he's gone."

Sara put a hand on his shoulder. "Maybe part of him is. But some of him will always be around here."

ABOUT THE AUTHOR

Russ Hall, who lives near Austin, Texas, is author of more than a dozen westerns, mysteries, and young-adult novels, as well as numerous short stories. He has also coauthored numerous nonfiction books. He served as an editor for major publishing companies, ranging from HarperCollins (then Harper & Row), Simon & Schuster, to Pearson. He won several awards, including the Sage Award, presented by the Barbara Burnett Smith Mentoring Authors Foundation—a Texas award for the mentoring author who demonstrates an outstanding spirit of service in mentoring, sharing and leading others in the writing community.